THE FATE OF THE FIVE KINGDOMS

SUMMONED TO ANOTHER WORLD AND FORCED TO
FIGHT THE DEMON KING

BOOK THREE

JAMES E. WISHER

SAND HILL PUBLISHING

PROLOGUE

Nora peeked out from behind a big pine tree. She couldn't hear the human knights that had been chasing her for what seemed like forever. They'd taken Tara away a few days ago. She didn't know where or why, only that the memory of her sister's screams woke her every time she fell asleep. Not that she slept much. The forest got cold at night, the ground was hard, and there were all kinds of noises.

She very much wanted to go back to the mansion. All she'd eaten since she got away was a few berries. Nora didn't usually eat a lot, but even for her, that was too little.

"Are you sure the brat came this way?" a gruff, angry voice said.

Nora slapped a hand across her mouth to keep from crying out. She'd been careful to sneak around like Grandma taught her.

"Something came this way," a second voice said. "Maybe it's her and maybe it's a woodchuck, but this trail's the only sign of life we've seen in hours. If you've got a better idea, I'm all ears."

"We ought to have a magic user with us," the first voice said. "A wizard would sniff the little shit out right quick."

A branch snapped and one of them cursed.

"If you want to go back and complain to the mistress," the second voice said. "I wish you the best of luck."

"No, I don't think I'll be doing that. I'll thrash around in these woods forever before I say a word of complaint to that woman."

"I knew you were clever."

The voices had gotten so close now that Nora hardly dared to breathe. She pressed against the pine tree so hard the rough bark scraped her back.

"Aw, shit." That was the second voice. It sounded like he was right on the far side of the pine. "The trail ends here. Some damn animal must've climbed the tree."

"So what now?" the first man asked. "I'm a knight, not a forester. We should've brought dogs."

A little tear leaked out of Nora's eye.

"No one planned for one of the kids to escape and your complaining isn't making this any easier. If you don't have anything useful to say, do me a favor and shut the hell up. Come on, let's backtrack a ways and see if we can find any other signs."

The two men stomped away and when she couldn't hear them anymore, Nora took her hand away from her mouth. Maybe one of her ancestors in Heaven was watching out for her. That had been too close.

Nora frowned. Why hadn't Heaven been watching out for Tara too? It wasn't fair. None of this was fair. They never bothered anyone.

She wanted to cry but refused. Once she got going, she'd

exhaust herself. Tara liked to tease her and call her a scaredy-cat. And maybe she was, a little. But now was the time to be brave, like Daniel.

When she thought of the gentle human that had played with them, Nora smiled. They'd all eaten lunch together that day and she'd asked him if he wasn't scared to fight the demon king. Daniel nodded and said he was scared, but that was okay. You were supposed to be scared when you had to do something dangerous. Being brave meant doing the scary thing anyway.

Nora had never thought about it that way before. She always thought that being scared was bad, but if even Daniel, the hero, got scared, maybe it was okay if she did too.

Yes, it was okay, but only if she was brave too. Nora wiped the tears from her eyes and forced herself to move.

She *would* be brave like Daniel and find someone to help her save Tara and find her grandmother. How such a miracle would come to pass she had no idea, but in her heart she believed it would and that was enough for now.

CHAPTER 1

T he warmth and crackle of the fire gave the inn's common room a homey feel that Danny liked. It was late summer and not especially cold in the evenings, but the heat still felt good. And he wasn't the only one that thought so. The room was crowded tonight. Three-quarters of the tables were occupied along with all but two of the bar stools. Best of all, the smell of roasting meat filled the air. The innkeeper had announced dinner would be ready shortly. In a world without clocks, Danny had no idea how long that might be, but he was looking forward to it all the same.

He yawned and stretched, leaning his chair back against the wall. His sword rested a few inches to his right, readily to hand. Peaceful as the town appeared, he wasn't about to get caught unarmed, not after what happened on his first mission. He shook his head and put that unpleasant experience out of his mind. Danny had already checked everyone he'd met and found no sign that anyone's mind had been tampered with. As far as he could tell, this town was exactly what it seemed.

And that suited him fine. He'd been running and fighting and killing for so long that a little break was most welcome.

He closed his eyes and let the murmur of voices lull him to the edge of sleep. Not all the way of course; he remained fully aware of everything going on and would sense any approaching corruption. No, he just wanted to clear his mind and enjoy the ambience.

His enjoyment lasted for all of five minutes before a faint clicking drew his attention to his tablemate. Eve was tapping her nail on the table as she chewed her lip. Clearly Adonael's high priestess wasn't enjoying the relaxed atmosphere as much as Danny. Eve wasn't much older than Danny's host body. At sixteen, she'd been chosen by the archangel to oversee his summoning to this world, ending his previous life on Earth.

Danny liked her anyway.

"Could you possibly calm down?" Danny asked. "We're safe for the moment. Let's savor it. Heaven knows it's not likely to last."

Eve peered at him through dark, bloodshot blue eyes. Looked like she hadn't been sleeping well. "Lady Shael should be here by now. We're only a couple days north of the capital. Making her report shouldn't have taken this long."

"You don't know what else might've come up." That sounded lame to Danny, and Eve's skeptical frown indicated she didn't think much of his reasoning either. The truth was he wanted his break to last as long as possible, so the longer Lyra took to rejoin them, the happier he'd be.

"Even if it did, she wouldn't leave us wondering. We should go check on her in the morning. There's one main road to the capital. We might meet her on the way."

That sounded like a horrible idea to Danny. He pitched his voice low. They were at a corner table well away from the nearest party, but he still didn't want anyone to hear him. "I can't exactly go to the royal castle. Someone's bound to recognize my voice no matter how much I changed my looks. The hero's dead and I'd like as many people as possible to keep believing that. Though since the cult of Ardent Lilly knows I survived, I suppose it's only a matter of time before word gets out."

"Come on, please? I'll go to the castle on my own. I can't stop worrying about her. With all the craziness in the world right now, you never know what might've happened. What if she's hurt and needs our help?"

Lyra was the most powerful person in the Five Kingdoms after Danny. The odds of her getting hurt, even if she was ambushed, were slim. Unfortunately, based on Eve's determined tone, he wasn't going to change her mind.

At last he sighed. "If I agree to leave in the morning—"

"Thank you!" Eve grabbed his hands, a big smile on her face.

He swallowed a second sigh. Looked like his break was coming to an end.

○

Nahia, the most loyal servant of the demon king, and dedicated priestess of Ardent Lilly, watched with disgust—and it took a lot to disgust her—as the replacement king stuffed his face from a spread of food large enough to feed an entire family. The gluttonous creature served an important role, at least for now. Should they find some way to replace it, Nahia would happily cut the monster's heart out and offer it to her mistress.

The fake king looked up, butter dripping from his face. "How much longer do I get to play this part? The food is excellent and the accommodations more than adequate. Since my family took up with the cult, this is easily the best job you've given us."

"You will play the part until the demon king returns to claim this land. How long that will take I have no idea. Recovering from her near death at the hero's hands will not be a speedy process. Even I, her most trusted aide, don't fully understand how the quadripartite resurrection works."

The fake king nodded then frowned. "Why do you call her demon king instead of queen? That never made sense to me."

Nahia shrugged, smoothed her black robe, and sat at the far end of the table. "The leader of the current demon lord linked to Demon King Castle is called the demon king; their gender is irrelevant. There's only one per cycle and they are the most powerful wielder of corrupt magic in the land. It has been so since the rise of the first demon king. My mistress will be the last to hold the title."

"You seem awfully confident given that she already died once."

Nahia's flawlessly arched eyebrows drew down and corruption gathered around her right hand. A black collar formed around the neck of the impostor and she squeezed. He gagged and clawed at his throat, eyes bugging further out of his head than any human's ever had.

When his face turned blue, Nahia decided her point had been made and released him. As he gasped for air she said, " You may be too useful for me to kill outright, but never forget that I can and will punish your foolishness. Do I make myself clear?"

"Absolutely! I meant no disrespect to you or the demon

king, may she rule forever. I simply wished to understand why you seem so confident in her. If I expressed my curiosity poorly, I offer my most heartfelt apology."

Nahia doubted the creature's sincerity, but at least it said the right things. "I'm confident because no demon king has ever survived a battle with the hero. My mistress is the first. She will return and end the cycle once and for all, claiming this world for Ardent Lilly."

The fake king nodded and went back to eating. Wise decision on his part. Whenever he said something that wasn't part of the role he was playing, it took all of Nahia's self-control not to kill him.

The worst part was that the fake's doubts were, partly, in the deepest recesses of her mind, echoed by Nahia. The plan was going largely as expected, but one major, unforeseen problem still stood in their way: the hero. He wasn't supposed to be resurrected as well. Two of her sister priest-esses had fallen by his hand already and she feared that the way things were going, more might join them.

An acceptable price to pay for ultimate victory, but a price none of them expected.

Someone knocked on the suite door and she stood. The illusion of the queen settled around her and she opened it. Outside waited one of her personal guards. "Do you have a problem?"

"No, Mistress," the guard said. "But it has been a couple days and no one has fed the prisoner or brought her water. While I am unfamiliar with elf-bloods in general, if you wish her to remain alive, it seems something must be done."

Nahia frowned. She'd been so focused on preparing for the upcoming ritual that she'd forgotten about her precious sacrifice. While the elf-blood wasn't strictly necessary to make it work, offering her and the brat would increase the magic's power considerably. Speaking of the child, the knights she sent should've returned with the second one long before now. How hard could it be for two grown men to find one kid?

"Mistress?"

She'd been staring off into space as she thought. It was never a good idea to let your subordinates see you distracted. Among demon worshippers, any sign of weakness could signal the leader was ripe for replacing. Not that the weakling before her would have any hope of defeating her even if she was sleepwalking.

"I'll deal with it. Return to your post."

He bowed and strode away.

Some of her sister priestesses would've punished him for daring to point out her potential mistake, but that, in Nahia's eyes, was a worse mistake. No one, save Ardent Lilly herself, was all knowing and all seeing. Having subordinates willing to speak was useful and, as long as they showed the proper respect, she encouraged them to do so.

But no matter, she had a prisoner to feed.

Nahia collected a roll and a carafe of water from the fake king's table before leaving the suite. The fake looked up at her but wisely stayed silent. This should be enough to keep the prisoner alive but still weak enough to be dealt with should she do something foolish. Not that she was likely to as long as they had her granddaughter as a hostage.

Smiling to herself, Nahia slipped out of the suite. Yes, there had been a couple of minor slipups, but all in all the plan was proceeding nicely. Once the ritual was complete, she wouldn't even need to fear the hero.

Lyra had known despair before. During a life as long as hers, it was inevitable. But as she sat in the dark of Castle Villipan's dungeon without so much as a rat for company, she wasn't sure she'd ever felt it as deeply as she did now. If it had only been her, Lyra wouldn't have been so miserable, but Tara was upstairs, under the control of those monsters. Her sweet, innocent granddaughter was suffering and she could do nothing.

Even worse, she had no idea where Nora was. At least she didn't appear to be a prisoner at the moment. Lyra took some comfort in that, assuming it didn't mean she was lying in a shallow grave somewhere.

No! She refused to think about the possibility. Nora was a clever girl. Surely she had escaped. Surely one of the children she'd sworn to protect was safe.

A creak was followed by a light that nearly blinded her for a moment. When her vision cleared she found the priestess who'd captured her standing in front of the bars. The darkly beautiful human smiled at her with cruel delight.

"I brought your feed. Best make it last. I won't be back for a couple more days." The woman tossed Lyra a roll and set a jug of water down outside the bars.

"How long do you mean to keep me locked up down here?" Lyra didn't expect an answer but felt the need to talk. An unusual thing for her.

To her surprise the priestess answered. "A little while longer. Ritual preparations are painfully time consuming and if you don't get them just right..." The woman shrugged. "Your granddaughter is a well-behaved little thing. You trained her well. Most children are less obedient than demons."

"Raised. The word you're looking for is raised, not trained. She's not an animal."

"That's where you're mistaken. All living things, no matter how intelligent, are, at some level, animals. You can train them with pain or sex or whatever they happen to want. If you do it right, you can control anyone without resorting to magic. Though the latter is far quicker and easier.

"Look at you. You could break out of your cell anytime you wanted to and we both know it, but you won't because you know what would happen if you did. See? No magic necessary."

The priestess turned and walked away, her harsh laughter seeming to echo in the dark long after she'd gone.

Lyra grimaced and took a bite of her meager repast. The roll was fresh at least. That was a welcome bonus. She hated how right the priestess was. These cells were nothing but stone and steel, neither an obstacle for her.

Just to prove it to herself, she went over to the bars of her door and bent them enough for the water jug to fit through. She drank then sighed as the cool water soothed her parched throat.

For now Lyra would play the good prisoner. But eventually they would take her out of this cell and bring her and Tara to wherever they planned to sacrifice them. That would be her moment to strike.

And when she did, she'd make the priestess pay for hurting her girls.

CHAPTER 2

Despite his wishes to the contrary, Danny found himself on the road again early the next morning. They were on the main trade route in the hopes of meeting Lyra partway to the capital. Merchant traffic hadn't gotten back to normal yet so he didn't worry about running into anyone.

He and Eve were off to check up on Lyra. No doubt she was stuck in some boring strategy meeting. It was a pretty standard thing, or so Danny's former CO had said. The higher-ups acted like talking about the problem meant they played some part in solving it.

Well, whatever. It wouldn't take too long for Eve to find out what was going on. For his part, Danny planned to hang out at Lyra's mansion. He wanted to make sure the girls were okay. Even if they were elves, they were still far too young to be left alone as often as they were. He wanted to suggest Lyra hire a babysitter, but it wasn't his place to butt in.

"Do you think we'll get to the city before dark?" Eve asked.

"I think so, but I'm not very familiar with this part of the kingdom. Or my body isn't at least. Based on our pace and the map in my head, I'd say we should be within sight of the walls by midafternoon at the latest. I do want to swing by the mansion to make sure she isn't spending one more day with her granddaughters." Speaking of, the trees of the little woodland behind the mansion were visible not far ahead.

"Good idea." Eve smiled at him. "No sense going all the way to the castle if we don't have to. The walk has been so nice you could almost forget demons were running around everywhere."

"Yeah, it's weird. We haven't seen anything nasty since Moreton and I don't trust it. A small army of demons and monsters doesn't just disappear. They have to be up to something and I'm sure we won't like it when we find out what."

"Don't be so negative. We're allowed to have good news once in a while."

"I'm not being negative, I'm being realistic." He paused and cocked his head.

He sensed life forces, two human and one not. Was that an elf? It wasn't Lyra, the presence was too weak and Danny knew the flavor, for lack of a better word, of her life force well enough to not mistake it for anyone else. This was similar but different.

Danny drew his sword. "Get behind me."

"What's wrong?" Eve asked as she obeyed.

"Not sure. Maybe nothing and maybe a lot. We'll find out in a minute."

To his considerable surprise, a little elf girl came running toward the road. He couldn't tell from this distance which one it was, but he had no doubt it was one of Lyra's granddaughters. Lumbering behind her were a pair of knights dressed in the Villipan colors. They were

14

armed but didn't have their weapons drawn. The men weren't especially fast, but their longer strides were closing the gap.

Why were they chasing the girl and where was her sister? Danny had no idea, but he meant to find out.

He strode forward.

The little girl spotted him. He watched fear and hope warring on her guileless face. At last she ran to him and clutched his leg.

"Help me. Please." She panted for breath. Up close it was clear she'd been through a rough time. Her dress was torn and filthy and her hair was a mess. The skin of her calves and hands was scratched and scraped.

"Don't worry, dearheart." Danny used the same term of endearment he remembered Lyra saying. "I won't let anyone hurt you."

She looked up at him with wide, dark eyes. "Daniel?"

Danny patted her head. "Stay with Eve and don't look this way."

With that final admonition he moved to intercept the now warily approaching knights. He hoped to deal with them without killing them, but when you had to fight, there were no guarantees.

They stopped a few feet apart. The knights didn't look much cleaner than the girl. One's mustache had twigs in it and the other's hair looked like a hedgehog. How long had they been trying to catch her?

"Hand the girl over and there'll be no trouble," Mustache said.

"The girl is a friend of mine and she's asked for my help. I'll be escorting her to her grandmother. You two look like you could use a bath and a good night's sleep. Leave her to me. I promise she'll be perfectly safe." As he was talking

Danny studied their minds. As he feared, they'd been tampered with.

"Those are not our orders." Hedgehog drew his sword and a moment later Mustache followed suit, sighing as he did so. "It's your bad luck that you chose to stand in the way of the finest knights in Villipan."

Danny had met some of the knights and he doubted these two buffoons were the cream of the crop. That said, they were just dupes being controlled by someone. It wasn't their fault they were weak-willed dimwits.

The knights charged.

They were pitifully slow. Danny shifted right and swung a hard left fist into Mustache's temple. He dropped like he'd been hit by a sledgehammer.

A quick parry turned aside an awkward thrust before Danny laid out Hedgehog with an uppercut that lifted him off his feet before crumpling him to the ground.

"Daniel!" The little girl came running toward him.

Danny sheathed his sword and scooped her up. She wrapped trembling arms around his neck.

"I was so scared, but I remembered what you said about being brave and I didn't give up."

Danny smiled. That conversation over lunch with the girls was one of his truly good memories from his time in this world. "You did well, Nora. Can you tell me what happened?"

She let go of his neck and wiped her eyes. "A group of knights came to the mansion and said they were bringing us to see Grandma at the castle. Grandma never brought us to the castle and always said to never go with anyone if she wasn't with us. Tara refused to lower the wards and slammed the door in their faces. I don't know what they did, but somehow they forced their way through the wards.

Knights shouldn't be strong enough to do that, but they did."

No, knights wouldn't be strong enough, but a high-tier demon would be. Danny had a sick feeling in his stomach but he didn't interrupt her story.

"We hid, but they found us. When we ran, Tara wasn't fast enough and they grabbed her. I made it out the back door and into the woods. I've been playing hide and seek with those two for days. I'm tired and hungry."

Danny opened his storage and pulled out a pouch of jerky. He offered a strip to Nora. "This is the best I can do for now. Once we get somewhere civilized I'll see about fixing you a proper meal."

Nora got busy chewing on the jerky like it was the best thing she'd ever tasted.

"What about the knights?" Eve asked.

"Yes, what about them. Someone used psychic magic to control their minds. If I dispel it, the caster will likely sense it. I'd like to avoid tipping our hand for the moment." Danny shrugged. "We'll lock them up in the mansion for now then continue on to the city. I'm not sure what's going on, but I've got a really bad feeling."

"This shouldn't be possible," Eve said. "These men are dressed in the king's colors. How could a demon or priestess make it into the city to take control of them?"

"That's an excellent question, one of many we need to sort out. For now, let's ditch our prisoners, find Nora some clean clothes and a proper meal, then we'll head for the capital."

"Going right to the castle doesn't seem like the best idea anymore," Eve said.

"It certainly doesn't. The problem will be finding someone we can trust, assuming such a person exists."

CHAPTER 3

Villipan City looked peaceful enough to Danny, at least from a distance. Guards patrolled the wall, four wagons were waiting to enter the north gate, and nothing was on fire. What more could you ask for?

Nora hadn't wanted to walk after her late lunch, so he ended up carrying her the whole way. Not that she was especially heavy. He'd given a vague explanation about his resurrection, claiming Heavenly magic was responsible. Nora asked no questions. She just seemed happy he was there to protect her. She also seemed more at ease with Danny holding her. After everything she went through, he was more than willing to offer what comfort he could. They'd left the knights in a magically induced coma back at the mansion. They wouldn't wake up for three days unless Danny died.

"I don't want to go to the city," Nora said. "Grandma always said we should stay away."

"That's generally good advice," Danny said. "However, with the mansion's wards shattered and no one to look after you, I'm afraid you're stuck with us. But don't worry, Eve and I will keep you safe."

"No creature of corruption can enter the Crystal Cathedral," Eve said. "Once we're inside, we'll be in no danger. Finding out what's going on at the castle is another matter. Going up to the front gate might not be wise."

"It's a terrible idea," Danny said. "But me sneaking in while using my stealth field is a much better one. You two can stay in the cathedral while I get the lay of the land. With any luck I might be able to rescue Lyra and Tara as well. If I can bust them out, we'll be in much better shape."

"Do you think you can save them?" Nora sounded so desperate it cut at Danny's heart, but he wouldn't lie to her.

"I don't know, but I'm going to give it my best shot."

About an hour before sunset they fell in at the rear of the line to enter the city. Not that three wagons loaded with summer vegetables was much of a line. The farmer driving the nearest wagon looked back at them.

Eve offered a friendly wave which he returned.

For his part, Danny checked the man for psychic magic and found he was clean. So far, so good.

When they were one wagon away Danny said, "Is it okay if I set you down? I want to have my hands free in case we run into trouble."

Nora nodded. "I'm okay now. Thanks for carrying me."

Danny lowered her gently beside him. It took only a moment to use an illusion to smooth the points of her ears. Nora looked human enough now. She held out her hand and Eve hastened to take it. Good, hopefully those two wouldn't get separated if things went to hell.

The final wagon trundled through the open gate and then it was their turn. He let Eve take the lead. No ordinary guard would dare question Adonael's high priestess. Just to be safe,

Danny checked all six men-at-arms and found them free from magical influence.

The squad commander, a man about Danny's father's age if the gray hair was any indication, stared at Eve as if he was seeing a ghost.

She smiled. "Good evening. I'm pleased to see that the capital is peaceful."

The guard sputtered for a moment then said, "High Priestess Carre, welcome home. No one sent word to expect you. We would've brought you to the front of the line. Are you here for the celebration?"

Eve shook her head. "No. A minor matter came up which made it necessary to return ahead of schedule. I didn't even know there was going to be a celebration. When is it?"

"Next Holy Day. I believe that's the day after tomorrow. The king has declared the war at an end. The demons and monsters have all scurried back to Fell Forest or wherever they came from. We haven't received word of an attack in weeks, thank Adonael."

Eve made the sign of the halo over her head. "Indeed. It's a relief to know the danger is past. May I enter?"

"Of course, but first, who do you have with you?"

Eve patted Nora on the head. "This is an orphan I'm taking to the cathedral. The gentleman behind me is Ronin, an adventurer I hired to guide me here and act as my bodyguard."

Danny held out his guild card and the guard gave it a cursory inspection. He was the high priestess's bodyguard after all; that was a strong endorsement of his good character.

"Shouldn't you be traveling with a larger entourage, Holiness?" The commander made a somewhat dismissive gesture toward Danny. "One adventurer seems insufficient."

"Since we made it here safe and sound, he was clearly more than sufficient." Eve's tone was sharp and the guard swallowed hard.

"I meant no disrespect, Holiness. Please, go right in."

Eve's bright smile returned. "Thank you."

When they'd left the gate behind Eve blew out a long sigh. "I hate lying."

"You didn't lie," Danny said. "Nora is technically an orphan, even though she's been adopted. Everything else you said was vague enough to be interpreted however the guard wanted. You handled the whole thing brilliantly, so relax."

"Thanks."

They walked through busy streets filled with calm, happy people. Everyone seemed to believe the war was over. Maybe they just wanted things back to normal and so didn't question the announcement. More likely they figured if word came down from the castle saying all was well, then it was.

Oh how wrong they were.

Other than a few shouts and friendly waves to Eve, they had no trouble reaching the area around the cathedral. Unfortunately, when they were a couple blocks away, things got more complicated.

"Hang on, you two. I sense some corruption. It looks like we've got some unwelcome company waiting for us. Let's get you out of sight then I'll take a peek."

"What is it?" Eve asked.

Nora stared at him with worried eyes.

"Not sure, but from the corruption in the air, I'm guessing a demon of some sort. Probably keeping an eye on the place in case you show up. Assuming you have no other way in, I'll need to take it out."

Eve shook her head. "I don't. The front door is the only

way in or out. I'm not sure why the angels made it that way, but they did."

Danny frowned. "What do you mean the angels made it?"

"Exactly what I said. Adonael sent angels here to use the power of creation to forge the Crystal Cathedral and connect it to the summoning circle. It's not something mortals could do."

Danny had serious doubts about the accuracy of her story given what he knew about summoning magic, but now wasn't the time for a theological debate.

He guided the pair to a nearby cafe and got them settled at a table. "I shouldn't be long."

"Be careful," Eve said.

Danny nodded. Being careful was a tricky thing when you were hunting for a demon. The thing that worried him was the summoner knowing he'd killed it and going on full alert. If that happened, sneaking into the castle would be much more difficult.

He left the cafe and stepped out into the street. A moment of concentration left him shaking his head. The corruption felt too diffused to be a demon. But if it wasn't a demon, he couldn't imagine what would be strong enough for him to notice. No doubt he'd find out soon.

Ambling along at a relaxed pace, Danny took his time approaching. The closer he got, the easier it was to feel the new magic. At a minimum he was certain no demon awaited him. That was a relief. A block from the cathedral Danny turned down a side street. He saw no one and sensed no hidden life forces.

Perfect.

His stealth field activated, turning him invisible and silent. Now, time to see what he could see.

Danny snuck closer, each step allowing him to analyze

the corruption in more detail. It looked like the magic formed a circle all the way around the cathedral. It didn't appear to be offensive. Maybe a detection ward? Several points of slightly thicker corruption drew his attention. He wasn't far from the nearest one now.

He turned down another side street and found a knight standing at attention, a thread of corruption running through him. Closer examination confirmed the knight was dead and a demon spirit was using his body. A thrall of some sort then. Though one without any outward signs of its transformation. He wished he was more surprised, but these dead things were useful for long-term guard duty. Since they looked human, the locals wouldn't pay much attention.

A full search of the perimeter confirmed a dozen thralls serving as anchors for the detection spell. No one would be able to enter the circle without the thralls and likely their master noticing. That might work to Danny's benefit. Assuming Eve was strong enough to shatter the ward.

It would be the perfect distraction to let him slip unnoticed into the castle.

CHAPTER 4

Eve sipped a cup of tea and tried not to think too hard about whatever sort of danger Daniel was walking into now. He had proven quite good at dealing with this sort of thing, but Eve still thought it was a shame that he kept having to. She'd never questioned Adonael's will, but the more she thought about the summoning ritual and what it meant to the heroes brought here against their will, the more she hated it. Saying they were acting for the greater good was fine, but sometimes the greater good was more of a lesser evil.

She peeked at Nora over the rim of her cup. The little elf-blood girl was a sweetheart. Watching her nibble on a sugar cookie was about the cutest thing Eve had ever seen. Daniel had so much bitterness and anger in him, and not unreasonably so, but you'd never know it when you saw him with Nora. He treated the girl with genuine kindness and warmth.

"Do you think Daniel can save Tara and Grandma?" Nora's question startled Eve out of her bleak thoughts.

"If anyone can, he can. Don't forget, he's Ronin now, at least when we're in public."

Nora's face scrunched up. "Why does he have a new name? Won't everyone be happy to know he came back to life?"

Eve wasn't sure how to answer her question. King Richard certainly wouldn't be since he was the one who ordered Daniel killed in the first place. She wasn't sure if the rest of the royal family was in on it but wouldn't be surprised if they were.

At last she settled on a polite lie. "I'm not sure why he doesn't want everyone finding out he's still alive, but I'm sure he has his reasons. It's enough for me to know he's okay."

Nora brightened. "Me too."

The conversation quickly ebbed. It was starting to grow a little awkward when the cafe door opened and Daniel walked in. He spotted them at once and waved to Eve. She dropped four small silver coins on the table and led Nora toward the exit.

Once they were outside and no one was around, Daniel explained what he'd found. When he finished, Eve wasn't sure if it was better or worse than finding a demon guarding the cathedral.

"Do you think you can break the ward?" Daniel asked.

"I don't know. Why?"

"I want you to act as a decoy for me. Run for the cathedral then break the ward once you're safe. The caster will be distracted, making it easier for me to sneak inside the castle. You'll be safe and I'll be free to act as I need to. It's only about a hundred-yard dash from the edge of the ward to the front door, so you shouldn't have any trouble making it before a thrall can reach you."

"Sounds risky," Eve said.

"You're not wrong. If you don't think you're up to it, I'll come up with another plan."

"I'm fast," Nora said. "I can run that far."

Daniel patted her on the head. "Such a brave girl. Your sister won't be able to call you a scaredy-cat after this."

Nora grinned. "She probably still will, but I'll know better."

Eve couldn't let herself be shown up by a little girl, even if that little girl likely was older than her. "I can do it. Will you meet us at the cathedral when you're finished?"

"If I can. A lot will depend on what the enemy does. At a minimum I'd like to bring Tara somewhere safe. That'll free up Lyra to act. I suspect she'll be...upset."

"Grandma will turn those knights that grabbed Tara into mincemeat," Nora said.

Daniel nodded. "I'll escort you most of the way. Give me ten minutes to get in place before you act."

"We can make it on our own," Eve said. "It's not that far."

"True, but if you go by the main road, you'll end up twenty paces from a thrall. You'll need a bigger head start than that. I'll show you the best spot."

The three of them took back alleys Eve hadn't known existed. Daniel never hesitated as he led them on their twisting path. Most interestingly, they didn't meet another person. Even in the rich part of the city, they should've run into someone. Were the people keeping their distance on purpose? Maybe it was an effect of the magic.

"Okay, this is as close as you can get." Daniel pointed down an alley. The cathedral was visible at the end of it. "Remember, give me about ten minutes before you cast. Longer is fine. I'll sense it when you start. Good luck."

With that, he faded from view and they were on their own.

Eve looked down at Nora, who was staring up at her. "We'll be okay. I might not be good at fighting, but I can make a barrier strong enough to stop any thrall. That'll keep us safe if we can't reach the cathedral. Okay?"

Nora nodded and took Eve's hand. "I hope Daniel can find Grandma and Tara."

"So do I. The important thing is for us to have faith in him. He's the hero, after all. If he can't save them, no one can." Eve thought she sounded pretty convincing. The truth was, Daniel no longer considered himself the hero. She took some comfort in the fact that, hero or not, he was a good person at heart who would help if he could. "Let's go."

The two of them got a running start and when they cleared the alley sprinted for all they were worth. Eve ignored everything save the cathedral's front door. It shamed her a bit that Nora had no trouble keeping up as they ran. She really needed to work out more.

Halfway to the door the corruption stirred.

Don't look, just keep running!

Pity she couldn't follow her own mental command. She flicked glances right and left. Thralls resembling human knights were running their way, far too quickly for her liking.

When they were ten yards away, Eve sent a mental command for the door to open. Even if Sister Rose sealed it, her authority would override the spell. Theoretically. She'd never tried it.

When they were three strides away the door started slowly swinging open. It was just wide enough when they arrived for Nora to run right through. Eve had to turn sideways, but she made it as well.

As soon as she was clear, she spun and slammed the door shut once more.

Lungs burning, Eve leaned against the door and took deep breaths. She checked on Nora but found the girl barely breathing hard. Eve swallowed a little growl. More exercise was definitely on the agenda, assuming they survived the next few days.

"Eve!" Sister Rose came running into the entry area from the chapel. "When I felt the sealing spell release I feared the worst. What are you doing here? It's dangerous to approach the cathedral."

Eve pushed away from the door. "I noticed. I think we need to exchange stories."

Nora let out a big yawn and rubbed her eyes.

"Would you like to lie down in my room?" Eve asked.

"I'm pretty sleepy," Nora said. "It's been a few nights since I slept in a bed."

"Come on. My bed is nice and soft." Eve held out her hand and Nora took it.

Sister Rose led them through the chapel. To Eve's considerable surprise, the crown prince, both princesses, and the king and queen of Forte were seated among the pews. What in the world were they all doing here?

She gave a little shake of her head. First things first. She'd put Nora to bed then see what was what.

The royals stared as she walked past, their eyes vacant and their expressions bleak. None of them spoke, which was a bit odd. They all had the blank look she'd seen on the faces of war survivors. Clearly whatever happened came as a major shock.

When they reached her room, Eve helped Nora change into one of her spare tunics then tucked her in. She was asleep before Eve reached the door. Poor kid. Despite being an elf-blood likely in her forties or fifties, Nora had the mind of an eight-year-old human. She'd done amazingly well so far, but it was no wonder she was exhausted.

Leaving her to sleep, Eve fell in beside Sister Rose and they headed back to the chapel.

"What happened?" Eve asked.

"Their story was a bit incoherent, but from what I gather, the king and queen were killed and replaced by demons. Only King Miles's warning allowed the rest of the royal family to escape. They made it here just ahead of the demons. We've been surrounded and unable to leave ever since."

"How did the people in charge explain that? I mean, this is the cathedral of Adonael. We're the spiritual heart of Villipan. When Holy Day arrives, the people need to come and pray. Not just for their souls, but to prepare for the next summoning."

"We've seen and heard nothing. No one has tried to approach the cathedral since the royals arrived. At least not until you got here."

Eve shook her head. None of this made any sense. "The city seemed calm. The guards at the gate showed me all due respect. If we were accused of some crime, surely they would've tried to arrest me."

Sister Rose shook her head. "I don't know what to tell you. Whatever's going to happen will likely happen on Holy Day. We'll see if the demons allow the people to come and pray. If they do, I'm not sure if we should open the doors. An assassin might slip in with the faithful."

"We will open our doors on Holy Day." Eve spoke in the firmest tone she could manage. "If anyone with evil intent tries to enter, they will face Adonael's wrath."

They reached the chapel and Eve went over to the royal

family. She still had a couple of minutes before she had to dispel the ward outside. Best to see what they had to say first.

She bowed and said, "Majesties, Sister Rose has explained some of the things that happened to you and I am most sorry for the ordeal you've had to face. Can you tell me anything about the enemy's plans?"

Prince—or was it King?—Florian raised his head and stared at her through bloodshot eyes. "My parents are dead, replaced by demons. None of the nobles are likely to believe me if I told them. It appears the knights are under the enemy's control and they have fully secured the castle. Meanwhile, we're trapped here, safe but powerless to do anything about the situation. Things could be worse, but not by much."

At the very least Florian appeared to have had the arrogance slapped out of him. That would be a good thing if he ever managed to assume the throne.

"Have faith, Majesty. Adonael won't abandon us in our hour of need. As long as we live, the battle isn't over."

Florian's smile held no hint of humor. "I want to believe you, but I have no faith left. Perhaps if Adonael were to show us a miracle. I can think of nothing less that would turn things in our favor."

Eve squeezed his shoulder and moved a couple benches down to King Miles. "It seems safety has been an elusive thing for you, Majesty. I'm sorry about that."

King Miles gave a little shrug. "The fortunes of war are what they are. While I wouldn't choose for myself and my family to live as refugees, it's better than the alternative."

"It certainly is. Where is the rest of your family, if you don't mind my asking? And didn't your kingdom's champion survive as well?"

"They're resting elsewhere. Alas, Dufour didn't survive our escape from the castle."

"That's unfortunate." Eve swallowed a sigh. "His magic would've been a huge help in the coming battle."

"Indeed, it's a painful loss. I wish I had more information to share. Since we fled Forte things have been happening so quickly I fear it's all a jumble."

Eve stood. "Perfectly understandable, Majesty. I wish I could do more to help, but for now, please continue to enjoy the cathedral's hospitality."

"You're a very kind young lady. Thank you."

Eve smiled and headed for the front door.

Sister Rose hurried to join her. "What are you doing?"

"Making a declaration of war. It's time to tell the enemy we won't go meekly into the night."

She threw the doors open. They were just a physical barrier; the cathedral's magic would keep anything corrupt out whether they were open or closed. Three of the thralls glared at her with glowing red eyes. They hadn't bothered to return to their hiding places, which struck her as a bad sign. Though a sign of what Eve couldn't say. For the moment, all that mattered was providing Daniel's distraction.

Eve placed her hand on the smooth crystal wall and focused on her connection to Adonael. Warmth rushed into her. When it felt like she was about to burst, she sent it out in a wave.

White light surged into the air. It hit the three thralls and burned them to ash. She sensed the others suffer the same fate. When the light faded, no sign of corruption remained. She'd done it.

She wobbled a bit as she pulled the doors closed and Sister Rose hurried over to support her. "Are you okay? I didn't know you could do something like that."

"I was only a conduit for Adonael's power. I doubt I could do it anywhere but here. We've made our opening statement. Now all we can do is wait and see how the enemy responds."

CHAPTER 5

D anny couldn't deny his anxiety when he left Eve and Nora to make their mad dash to the cathedral, but in the end, he couldn't be in two places at once. They had their part to play and he had his. So he hurried through the streets, silent and invisible, like a ghost among the living. He hardly needed the magic. The streets were virtually empty. It was approaching sunset, but still, he expected to find a few more people out and about.

Not that it mattered for his purposes. The rich and powerful of Villipan could do whatever they wanted in the evening. His goal was the castle looming just ahead.

As he approached the outer wall Danny scanned the area for new wards and corruption. And found nothing. Everything looked exactly as it did when he left to fight the demon king. The enemy probably hadn't had time enough to make many changes. What little his host knew about wards suggested the process for creating large-scale permanent ones took months and required artifacts to act as anchors. Not a speedy process by any means.

He paused a few yards from the main gate. The squad of guards on duty all had their minds altered. The archers on the battlements were the same. On the plus side, they still looked human. If he killed whoever enchanted them, they should fall unconscious. Then it would be up to the healers to repair the mental damage.

Two quick strides combined with an ether enhanced leap carried him up and over the wall. Danny landed silently in the courtyard then listened for any sign his arrival had been noticed. From the lack of alarm, he decided it hadn't.

Now it was a matter of waiting for Eve's distraction.

With nothing better to do while he waited, Danny walked around the courtyard. It was quiet, which meant the smith was done for the day. The servants must have called it a night as well. Only the four guards outside the keep entrance were visible. Of course they'd all had their minds altered as well.

Danny couldn't help wondering how many demons were inside. From out here, all he could sense was a vague hint of their corrupt presence. He had to assume a handful at minimum to keep everyone under control. No, this had to be an important mission; he'd best assume a large force was on hand. Better to be overprepared than under.

He slipped closer to the entrance and waited. Shouldn't be long now before Eve made her move. Hopefully she'd be strong enough to do what needed to be done.

The answer came a few minutes later when divine white light exploded out of the temple, washing over everything nearby. He hadn't expected such an impressive display. Being in her home cathedral must've had a positive effect on her magic. The person in charge here couldn't have missed a spell on that scale.

Five minutes passed, then ten. Apparently noticing it and

being willing to come out for a closer look weren't the same thing. So much for his brilliant plan. Looked like he'd have to take a more aggressive approach.

Danny went over to the empty smithy but dismissed it at once. Made of stone and with a tile roof, there wasn't enough flammable material to work with. The stable, on the other hand, would be perfect.

He opened the stable door then all the stalls. Some might call him soft hearted, but killing innocent animals wasn't his style. Besides, a bunch of terrified horses running around the courtyard would be nearly as big of a distraction as the fire.

A simple fear spell set the horses to neighing and stomping before they ran out. That done, he tossed a small fireball into the hay loft. It went up as quick as you please.

As he hoped, the guards on duty started banging on the keep door shouting for help. Danny moved closer. The door slammed open and a squad of guards along with a bunch of servants came rushing out.

Danny slipped in, unnoticed amidst the chaos. He hurried down busy halls, hugging the wall to make sure none of the panicked servants ran into him. After a couple of familiar twists and turns he finally found a spot free from people.

Now, where were Tara and Lyra? The two elf-bloods, with their magical natures, should stand out like a lit torch at midnight. Opening himself fully to the ether, Danny let his awareness drift through the castle. It didn't take long to find the two sparks he sought. Lyra was downstairs, likely in the dungeon. Danny had never seen it himself, but where else would it be?

Tara was on the second floor. A dark presence was far too close to the little girl for comfort.

No way would Lyra do anything to put her grand-daughter in danger. Which meant Danny had to free Tara first. That wouldn't be his preference since escaping from the second floor would be far easier than escaping from the dungeon. But he'd figure something out.

He knew the layout of the castle well enough to make his way to the nearest staircase without getting lost. A few steps from the top, he froze. A weak source of corruption was just to one side of the exit. Felt like a thrall or maybe a weak demon. His stealth field should keep him hidden from its magical senses. He debated taking it out, but in the end decided against it. Nothing could be allowed to give away his presence.

At the top of the steps Danny poked his head out. Sure enough, a knight that had been transformed into a thrall waited right where he expected. The creature never even looked his way as he snuck down the hall toward where he sensed Tara.

He passed one closed door after another until he stood in front of the right one. She was inside, in what he assumed was a guest bedroom. The dark presence was only a few feet away from her. Far too close for comfort. As soon as he opened the door, the demon or whatever it was would realize someone was here, even if it couldn't see him.

Danny opened his storage and pulled out the ethersword, careful to wrap it in a thick barrier to hopefully prevent the enemy from sensing the mithril. He was only going to get one shot at this.

Crouching in front of the door, he eased the hilt against it. With his left hand he scratched the wood, like a cat trying to draw someone's attention. He didn't know if the castle had any cats—he hadn't seen any during his stay—but it seemed like something would have to deal with any mice that snuck in.

He repeated the sound twice more, getting a little louder

each time. Come on, you stupid demon. Don't you want to pet the kitty?

On the third scratch he sensed the dark presence approaching. Danny tightened his grip on the ethersword. When the creature was right in front of the door, he activated the blade.

The beam of pure white energy shot out, piercing the wood like it was nothing.

Danny sliced down, then across. The door fell in four pieces. Beyond it, one of the sexy nuns had been carved into matching pieces. Tara sat on the bed staring at the ruined door and dead woman.

Shit! He'd probably traumatized the poor kid.

Still, they had no time for coddling. He ended his stealth field and deactivated the ethersword. "Tara? It's time to collect your grandmother and get out of here. Can you move?"

She stared at him in obvious confusion. "Who are you?"

"It's Daniel. Nora told me what happened. I came to free the two of you."

The sound of pounding footsteps filled the air.

"No more time to talk." Danny hurried over and scooped her up. Back in the hall he reactivated his stealth field and ran for a different set of stairs. She didn't fight him at least. Thank goodness for small favors. Carrying a struggling kid would make this so much harder.

Halfway to the second staircase Danny had to dodge around a squad of knights that came barreling around the corner. He sensed no corruption which meant they were human and only under the demon's mind control. That made them harder to sense.

As they ran past, Tara clung to him even tighter. He would've liked to offer her words of comfort, but didn't dare risk someone hearing his voice. The stealth field was powerful magic, but it wasn't perfect.

When it was safe to move, he hurried on. But not for long. A squad of six knights was guarding the stairs. He hesitated. They weren't a threat to him, but they also weren't the real enemy. The problem was, he couldn't take them out gently and protect Tara.

Screw it. He'd power through and hope for the best.

"Hold on," he whispered.

Tara squeezed his neck in response.

Steeling himself, Danny shifted the magic of the stealth field into a solid barrier and charged. The knights had no time to react before he hit them like a cannon ball. Men went flying in every direction, raising a horrible racket as their armor slammed into the ground and walls. One unfortunate fellow ended up rolling down the stairs in front of Danny. When he hit the floor at the bottom he didn't stand back up.

Danny jumped over the body and kept going, shifting back to the stealth field as he did so. Part of him wanted to head straight for the exit, but if he didn't rescue Lyra now, they might well kill her once they lost their leverage. A month ago he might've been fine with that. But now all he could think about was having to tell the girls their grandma was dead. He wanted to do few things less.

And so he turned toward the entrance to the dungeon. Assuming he could reach Lyra, hopefully they could figure something out together.

W hen the thralls she'd set to guarding Adonael's cathedral were destroyed, Nahia leapt to her feet. It seemed like the priests had finally grown enough spine to act. Took the weakling cowards long enough.

The lack of any follow-up action made no sense. Surely they had more power than that. When a minute passed, then two, she decided it was safe enough to return to her nap. She'd been resting in the royal chambers. The stress of the ritual preparations left her exhausted every evening. Some people might think a demon ritual was best prepared for at night, but they were idiots. The intricate spell weaving was much easier when you had daylight to work with.

Activating it, on the other hand, would happen at night. At midnight in fact, two days hence on the night of the new moon. She was three-quarters of the way finished and nothing could be allowed to interfere.

Halfway to the couch, shouts of alarm rang out. With a little growl she stalked over to the door and yanked it open. "Find out what's going on," she said to the guards outside.

Wonderfully obedient slaves that they were, both men ran off to take a look.

Nahia slammed the door closed and opened herself to the ether. Enhancing all of her senses, she could hear no sounds of battle. A faint wisp of smoke reached her. Was the city on fire? No, that would've put out more smoke than she smelled. Something smaller then.

She ground her teeth. Why couldn't she extend her sight like the wizards? It was an annoying limitation. Ardent Lilly was omnipotent, surely her mistress could grant the ability.

Nahia put such thoughts out of her mind. Insulting her mistress, even in the most modest way, wasn't a good idea. Demon lords weren't only omnipotent, they were also vengeful. If there was one thing Nahia didn't want, it was to draw her wrath.

"What is all the noise?" The false king emerged from the royal bedchamber.

"Something's on fire."

He rubbed his face. "And this requires you to slam the door why?"

"Because I'm annoyed. I can either slam the door or my whip into your back. Which do you prefer?"

The false king winced. "This is why I hate working with demon worshippers. So much anger and violence. We're winning, for hell's sake, can't you enjoy it?"

"You work with us because you have no other reasonable options. It's not like the forces of Heaven have any use for your kind."

A knock sounded and the door opened a fraction. One of the guards stuck his head in. "The stable caught fire, Mistress. The guards and servants are working to put it out now. There's no danger to any other buildings."

"How did the stable catch fire?" the false king asked.

That was an excellent question, one Nahia would like the answer to as well.

"A lantern might have fallen over," the guard said. "It happens from time to time."

The false king stared at him. "Why would the lanterns be lit when it's still daylight outside?"

The guard looked like he very badly wanted to run away. "I don't know, Majesty."

"Put the castle on full alert," Nahia said. "If the fire didn't start by accident then someone set it. Probably as a distraction to sneak inside. Whoever was stupid enough to do that will regret their decision for what remains of their very short life. I'm going to check on the hostage. Richard, stay here."

"My very plan," the fake king said.

She snarled and stalked out of the suite. Miserable coward, just like all his kind. Pity they were so useful. If she hadn't had orders to the contrary, Nahia would've very much enjoyed killing him in the slowest and most painful fashion imaginable.

A mental command summoned her personal guards. Thralls and normal humans would be pretty much useless, but they might slow down whoever was here long enough for her to catch up to them. She had a sick feeling in the pit of her stomach.

The one most likely to succeed in sneaking into the castle was the hero. If he was here, Nahia wasn't sure she wanted to catch up to the man. He'd already killed a number of her sisters. And unlike the demon king, resurrection wasn't an option for them.

Her guards joined her at the top of the steps and the group hurried toward the unused bedroom where they kept the girl locked up. One of her under-priestesses was on duty at all times just in case. Nahia doubted the whelp of an elf-blood would be able to escape a locked room on her own. But given the value of her blood as well as her usefulness in keeping Lyra in line, she had wanted to take no chances.

They rounded a corner and she immediately spotted the slabs of a ruined door lying in the hall. Two of the guards ran ahead.

As soon as they reached the door one of them looked back. "She's gone and Lady Obelisk is dead."

Nahia slammed her fist into the wall with enough force to crack the stone. "We didn't pass them on the way and there are only two staircases. Come on!"

She sprinted down the hall toward the second staircase. They couldn't have gotten far. Even if it was the hero, she had to try and stop him. Her punishment would be far worse if she tried and failed than if she did nothing.

As she ran, Nahia sent a mental command to all those under her control. *Muster at the dungeon entrance. The enemy is headed that way. Stop him at all costs, but do your best not to kill the child.*

If they killed the brat she'd be in just as bad a shape when Lyra went on a rampage. She growled. This was why Nahia hated taking hostages. So many things could go wrong. It was always better to kill everyone and be done with it. If only elf blood wasn't so damned useful!

Around another corner they found a squad of guards sprawled on the floor. It looked like they'd been scattered by a giant's club. Clearly the intruder had come this way. She noted in passing that they all survived. Pathetic as they were, they could still be sacrificed later to summon demon spirits.

At the bottom of the steps Nahia turned right, toward the entrance to the dungeon. There was only one way to access the second subfloor dungeon; that's where she'd make her stand.

CHAPTER 6

Danny found the stairs to the basement blessedly free of guards. He slipped down the steps and at the bottom set Tara down before ending his stealth field. Continuous use of so much magic had left even Danny worn out. He needed some time to catch his breath and recover.

The dim light filtering down the staircase didn't show much. A stone hallway ran past a number of rooms with closed doors, none of which looked appropriate for a prison. Maybe the dungeon part of the basement was further in.

The absolute silence confirmed they were alone down here. He couldn't sense any corruption either. Lyra's life force was still a little ways away, but it felt strong. Danny couldn't imagine why they didn't kill her, but clearly whoever was in charge around here wanted Lyra for something.

Tara tugged on the hem of his tunic.

Danny looked down at her. "What's on your mind, kiddo?" He kept his voice low on the off chance someone was walking by upstairs. He avoided summoning a light for the same reason.

"Is Nora really okay?"

Danny nodded. "She really is. I found her running from some knights. She's with Eve at the cathedral now."

"How come you're alive? And where's your hair?"

Danny grinned and gave her a heavily edited version of what happened after Lyra killed him. "It was a miracle from Heaven. Now we have to make the most of it. Let's find Lyra so we can escape this place."

Tara nodded. "I want to go home."

"I know you do, but that might not be possible for the time being. Too many evil people know where you live and they all want to use you and your sister to control Lyra. That's not a great outcome for a lot of reasons. But we'll sort this mess out eventually, never fear."

She hugged him. "I'm glad you're okay."

Danny patted her head. "Me too, kiddo, me too."

After a ten-minute rest Danny figured they'd best move on. No one had shown up looking for them, which struck him as odd. Surely the demons' leader was smart enough to figure out he'd be going to rescue Lyra as soon as he freed Tara. But apparently not.

Never one to look a gift horse in the mouth, Danny set out down the corridor. He held Tara's hand with his left and the deactivated ethersword with his right. The stealth field seemed pointless since no one was around and it would only drain his strength in any case.

His magical senses led him unerringly deeper into the basement toward Lyra's unique life force. The further they went, the more the lack of cells bothered him. Where the hell was the actual dungeon?

The answer came a minute later when he realized he

needed to go down to reach Lyra. There had to be another level below this one. Since they hadn't run into any guards, they must be protecting another floor altogether. That might work out to Danny's advantage, as long as he moved quickly.

Homing in on Lyra's presence, he inched along until he stood right above her. He ended up right in the middle of another hall. Well, whatever. This wasn't his floor.

He took two strides back, lit the ethersword, and drove it into the floor. It made no sound beyond the faint crackle of disintegrating stone as he cut a two-foot-diameter hole. A telekinetic hand caught the plug of stone and set it aside. When he looked down he found Lyra staring up at him.

Danny grinned. "Going my way?"

Tara hurried over beside the hole. "Grandma!"

"Shh!" Danny and Lyra said at the same moment.

Someone shouted and Lyra said, "They're coming."

"Then let's get the hell out of here." Danny reached down and Lyra jumped. Her narrow shoulders fit easily through the hole. "You okay?"

"Hungry and angry in roughly equal measure, but uninjured."

Tara latched on to Lyra's leg. "I was so scared, Grandma."

Lyra picked her up and hugged her as Danny led the way back to the exit. He wasn't sure if getting out was going to be as hard as sneaking in, but at least the two people he was trying to keep safe were free. More or less.

"Did you find my ring?" Lyra asked.

"What ring?"

"My key ring. I can't access the hero's armor or sword or any of the other items I have stored away without it."

"No, I didn't come across it. We can find it later. Right now we need to retreat and meet up with Eve at the cathedral. Nora's waiting for you."

"You found her?" Lyra asked. "Where?"

"She was running from some knights. Apparently she'd been hiding from them for a few days in the woods behind the mansion. She's at the cathedral. Seemed like the safest place."

"It certainly is," Lyra said. "I appreciate you looking after my girls. I know you didn't have to."

"Whatever our differences of opinion—" he smiled faintly at the euphemism "—I have no desire to see anything happen to innocent children. Damn it! I should've grabbed you a sword. Wait."

He opened his storage and pulled out the sword he'd taken from the bandit. It was good steel if nothing remarkable.

"Thanks." Lyra belted it on.

Half a minute later they reached the stairs to the ground floor. Danny sensed numerous sources of corruption waiting for them at the top.

"It appears our arrival has been anticipated."

"The... person in charge isn't stupid. It's one of the priestesses we keep running into."

"That doesn't surprise me. I ran into another one guarding Tara. She won't be a problem. You two stay down here. I'll clear a path."

"I'll join you," Lyra said. "I'm not that weak."

Danny shook his head. "If any of them make it past me, you need to protect Tara. Don't worry, I can't sense anything especially powerful. I can take them."

Lyra's face twisted as she thought. Danny could almost hear the gears turning in her head. Finally she said, "Alright, but be careful. Underestimating a demon is a good way to end up dead."

"You don't have to tell me."

With that he lit the ethersword and strode toward the steps. Halfway to the top he increased his physical enhancement. The first thing he saw was a black-armored knight reeking of corruption.

Danny kicked off the step with enough force to shatter the stone. A powerful slash bisected the black knight at the waist, his armor not slowing the blade in the least.

He spun and cut down a pair of approaching thralls with a single blow. After that, things became a blur of carnage. The ethersword severed limbs and heads with equal ease. Danny wove through the demons' clumsy attacks like a mongoose fighting a cobra. They might as well have been moving in slow motion.

His only regret was having to kill a handful of still-human knights who attacked along with the thralls. It was a shame, but you had to do what you had to do.

At last he stood alone at the top of the stairs. There was no sign of a priestess or any high-level demons. Just weak trash. The slaughter struck him as pointless, but he wasn't about to complain.

"We're clear, but it's not pretty up here."

Lyra climbed up, holding Tara, who had her face buried in her shoulder. Good, this was the sort of scene that would leave a kid with nightmares for the rest of her life.

"We good to go?" Danny asked.

Lyra's hesitated, but after a few seconds she said, "Yes. As you said, we can return and find my ring later. I want to take her somewhere safe."

Danny led the way to the exit. The heavy doors were wide open and there was no sign of the guards. He paused long enough to slice through the hinges, sending both doors crashing to the ground. That would make getting in much easier next time. The wall was equally abandoned and no force of soldiers waited in the courtyard to oppose them. It was still twilight out. He would've sworn he'd been in the castle for hours.

"You ever have the feeling your host is eager for you to go home?" Danny asked.

"I suspect you're exactly right. No doubt when we come back, we'll find a nasty surprise waiting for us. For now, I'm happy to grant their wish."

They left the castle behind and made the short walk to the cathedral. The door was shut when they arrived, so Danny knocked.

A few seconds later a weary-looking Eve opened the door. Her wan face looked less healthy than after she helped heal all those villagers. She stepped aside so they could come in then fell in beside Danny.

"You look like hell," he said.

"Channeling so much of Adonael's power took a toll on me. But I'll be fine. Just need a good night's sleep. I'm glad you got them out okay."

"Me too. How's Nora?"

"Sound asleep in my bed. Poor thing looked done in."

"I'll lay Tara down beside her," Lyra said. "She dozed off halfway here."

"It's in the back. I'll show you."

Danny held back as the ladies hurried through the chapel. The only other person present, Prince Florian, sat in the front pew, head bowed, as if seeking divine inspiration. Danny hoped he got it. How Villipan was going to recover from this Danny had no idea, but it would fall to the prince to see it done.

Not wanting to interrupt his prayer, or talk to him for that matter, Danny settled in a pew at the very back of the room. He didn't think Lyra would want to return to the castle until morning. At least he hoped she wouldn't. He'd used enough magic for one day and he suspected she'd need sleep and food before she was close to being at her best.

Florian straightened and made the halo symbol over his head. He slowly turned to face Danny, who waved but didn't bother getting up. To his near shock, the little shit didn't take offense. Instead the prince walked back and sat in the pew in front of Danny.

"Who might you be, sir?" Florian asked.

Danny debated telling him the truth then discarded the idea. "Ronin. I'm an adventurer in the employ of Lady Shael. I snuck into the castle and freed her. Stealth magic is my specialty."

"You must be very talented to sneak into a castle full of demons. If I had to guess, I'd say you were younger than me."

Danny shrugged. "Letting your client die is bad business. Plus, I like kids, so rescuing the little one was worth doing."

"And what are your plans now?" Florian asked.

"Like I said, I'm under contract with Lady Shael. Whatever she decides we need to do next, I'll back her up. She hasn't told me anything yet. Given that she'd been locked in a cage for the last few days, I imagine her priorities will be food and sleep."

"If she can sleep, then I envy her. I haven't been able to sleep more than an hour or two at a time since we fled the castle."

"That must have been tough," Danny said.

Florian nodded and looked away as if lost in thought. "It was the most difficult thing I've ever done by a fair margin. Though I'm sure many would say it was the first difficult thing I've ever done."

Danny had no idea how to respond to the bitter remark and so stayed silent.

"Forgive me, I've been a bit maudlin since Father was killed. Not a good look for the new king."

"I expect a king can look any way he wants. Certainly no one can fault you for feeling poorly after losing your parents. If you'll forgive the question, how are your sisters holding up?"

Florian snorted a short, humorless laugh. "We've never been especially close. Certainly not so close that they would confide anything in me. Perhaps that's why I wanted to talk to you, an adventurer with no particular standing. It felt safe."

"Happy to be of service, Your Majesty." Danny thought he sounded pretty convincing. The truth was he couldn't have cared less about Florian's mental state. The obnoxious twit might have been humbled by his recent brush with death, but he was still a worthless turd as far as Danny was concerned.

Thankfully Lyra and Eve chose that moment to return to the chapel. They marched right down the aisle to join Danny and Florian. Danny slid over and Eve sat beside him. Lyra remained standing, arms crossed, and looking for all the world like she wanted to kill someone. Which she probably did. Pity none of them were on hand.

"Lady Shael," Florian said. "A full report would be much appreciated."

"What's the last piece of news you received?" Lyra asked.

Florian frowned. "The last formal meeting I recall was when Miles arrived and told us about the attack on Forte. Sounded like it was a nightmare."

"I imagine it was," Lyra said. "So far we've uncovered two —three, counting the capital—locations where priestesses of Ardent Lilly have taken control of the local populace."

She filled him in on the farming village as well as Moreton.

"So Duke Morel is dead." Florian didn't sound especially upset. Hardly surprising given Danny's brief interactions with the family. "I suppose Alban will take over when he's recovered. We've always gotten along well. It will be good to have one sure ally when the time comes for the conclave of nobles to recognize my succession."

"Assuming any nobles survived to attend," Lyra said. "We still have no idea how many other towns have been taken over."

"What an alarming thought. I assume you have a plan?" Florian's desperation was as pitiful as it was understandable.

"Once I'm recovered, we'll sweep the castle and clear out any remaining demons. When that's done, the priority has to be checking the other nobles and seeing if any of them have been subverted. Villipan won't be safe until that's done."

"What about the other kingdoms?" Eve asked. "If the demons are doing this here, they must be doing the same elsewhere, don't you think?"

"Maybe they'll just wipe them out like they did Forte," Danny said. "Also, what about those black stones and the portals?"

Lyra nodded. "It's quite likely they tried to wipe out the other capitals. Their objective is the cathedral. If they can control Villipan and destroy the other four kingdoms, the demon king will be able to walk in and smash the place unopposed. As for the rest, I don't know. My hope is that, like with Moreton, we'll find the stones where we find the priestesses."

"What a cheery thought." Florian stood. "I believe I'll try to sleep. You have my permission to do whatever you think necessary. Good luck."

So saying, the prince ambled off into the rear of the church.

When he'd gone Lyra said, "He's a good deal less bossy than I'd feared. Nothing like getting slapped in the face with reality to improve your attitude."

"Yeah, reality has a way of doing that." Danny stood. "What are the odds of getting a hot meal and a soft bed?"

Eve smiled. "I can arrange the food, but our spare bedrooms are all occupied by royals. I fear the best I can offer is a spot on the floor."

"Sold." Danny was so tired he figured he could sleep just about anywhere. And from the sounds of it, he'd need all his strength for tomorrow.

CHAPTER 7

Nahia relaxed when she sensed the hero's presence fade. She'd been fairly confident he wouldn't want to risk a fight with the kid tagging along, and it turned out she was right. But Nahia harbored no illusions about the long term. This was a temporary reprieve at most. She needed to buy one more day. Just one more day and the ritual would be complete. If she could make her plan work, this would be the perfect opportunity to secure victory.

Emphasis on *if*. Everything would have to go perfectly. And the sooner she got started, the better.

First she sent a mental command to all the humans under her control telling them to return to their homes until she recalled them. Next she ordered all her followers to join her in the royal suite. She had orders to give and they needed to be carried out quickly.

"So what now?" the imposter asked. He'd been standing there so quietly she'd almost forgotten about him. Another one of his people's skills. It was lucky for everyone they were both rare and lazy. Had it been otherwise they might have taken over the world by now.

"I'll explain when the others arrive. Though I'm sure you'll be disappointed, your days of having to pretend to be king are over."

He shrugged. "I knew this would be a short assignment. What about the others?"

"They will need to stay in place until the demon king returns. That was the arrangement," Nahia said, her voice sharp. "You all accepted knowing it might be years before her return."

"I'm not complaining, just confirming. You really need to work on your temper."

He was spared a scathing reply by the timely arrival of her now-much-diminished entourage. There was a succubus, a squad of blackguards, and her final surviving underpriestess. Not a group to strike terror into the hero. Luckily, if her plan worked, they wouldn't have to fight him at all.

"What are we going to do, Mistress?" Bella, her underpriestess, asked. "Surely the hero will be coming at first light."

"I have no doubt that both he and the elf-blood will be here far too soon. That's why you'll be serving as a distraction." Nahia took a ring out of her pocket. "You will take this and flee as far and as fast as you can from the city. Go northwest. Make it look like you want to reach Demon King Castle. That will make your movement more believable."

Bella reached for the ring with a trembling hand. "What is it?"

"The elf-blood's key ring. She'll be able to sense it getting further and further away as you flee. Hurry now, you should be able to make ten miles by morning, hopefully more. I need you to buy me a day and a half."

Bella chewed her lip but nodded. It wasn't like she had the option of disobeying. "I'll use shadow wings until the sun comes up. I'll travel even faster with them."

Nahia smiled. That spell took a high toll on the user's body and only worked at night. It was a good idea and she was pleased Bella had offered to use it.

Bella bowed and hurried out of the suite.

"The rest of us will hide in my pocket dimension when we sense the hero's approach. All he'll find is an empty castle and a fleeing priestess."

Victory would be hers. Nahia could feel it. And with victory would come greater power. What priestess could ask for more?

◯

Danny had been sound asleep, sprawled out on the chapel floor, when something passed through his ward. He sat up, blinding light filling the area at his mental command. As soon as he saw King Miles, arms raised to protect his eyes from the sudden light, Danny relaxed and reduced the spell's intensity.

"Evening, Majesty," Danny said. "Couldn't sleep?"

Miles shook his head, his long, uncombed hair flopping every which way. "I apologize for waking you. I thought I was being quiet."

"You were, but when you passed through my defensive ward you triggered a spell that wakes me up and renders me instantly alert. Very useful when you have to camp out at night."

"You used such a spell inside Adonael's cathedral? Not very trusting, are you?"

Danny grinned. "Not especially, but this was more habit

than worry about getting attacked. I set the ward when I'm staying at inns as well. I find I can't fall asleep if it isn't active. It's an adventurer thing."

"I haven't known many people in your line of work. It seems like a dangerous way to make a living."

"You're right, but the money's good and I appreciate the freedom. I can go where I want, do what I want, and I'm only beholden to my employer. At the moment that would be Lady Shael. As employers go, she's not the best one I've ever dealt with. Since I hired on, she's changed the terms of the contract twice." Danny shrugged. "She also increased my compensation twice, so I guess I can't complain too much. Did you need something or are you just out for a midnight stroll?"

"The latter I suppose. Given all that's happened, I have a hard time sleeping. I thought a quiet walk around the chapel would soothe me. I hoped I might receive a vision from Adonael."

"Eve said she'd only gotten two and she's the high priestess. Probably best not to get your hopes up."

"I suppose not. I'll take my meandering to the back passages so you can sleep." Miles looked around, a little frown creasing his lips. "Where's Lady Shael? I assumed she'd be out here as well."

"She decided to camp out beside the girls' bed. Feeling a bit overprotective given everything that happened. Can't say I blame her."

"Indeed. I consider myself incredibly lucky that my entire family made it out of the capital. Well, I'm sure you have a busy day tomorrow. I'll let you go back to sleep."

Miles left and Danny lay back down on his bedroll. Didn't seem like the king recognized him despite their meeting at the royal feast. If it hadn't been to his advantage, he might've been offended.

Danny restored the ward and doused his light. As he lay awake, staring into the dark, he couldn't help wondering why Miles lied about half the things he said. Probably a noble thing, trying to say what he thought Danny wanted to hear. Earth politicians had similar tendencies.

Some things, it seemed, were universal.

CHAPTER 8

The sun was barely peeking over the city walls when Danny and Lyra set out for the castle. The streets were empty, which seemed strange until he remembered this was the wealthy part of town. They probably didn't wake up until later. He could sense people's life forces inside the buildings which did wonders to relieve his anxiety.

When they rounded the corner that led to the castle, he frowned. There wasn't a guard in sight. The walls were abandoned and the gate wide open.

"What the hell?" Danny asked.

Lyra shook her head. "I don't know. I'm sure a few demons remained when we left yesterday. Perhaps they fled knowing we'd be back today."

"That's not a very demonic thing to do. Usually the stupid things keep trying to kill us until we've destroyed them all. I always assumed they were trying to score a lucky hit."

"Demons have no fear. Even if they're destroyed, unless

they're purified by mithril, they'll reform in their master's hell ready to begin again. It makes them difficult to fight."

"Among other things." Danny held up the ethersword. "Does this count as mithril? The blade is pure ether so I wasn't sure."

"I'm not either. The only person who could answer your question with certainty is one of the long-dead half-elves. My guess is no, unless you beat them to death with the hilt.

Danny's smile held no hint of humor. "I've done that a couple times. This thing is the best pair of brass knuckles ever."

They entered the courtyard and nothing tried to kill them. The only thing of note was the half-burned-down stable. Danny was impressed they'd saved as much of it as they did. What he couldn't figure out was where the horses ended up. Hopefully someone took them out of the city.

"I sense no corruption," Lyra said.

Right, time to focus. Danny opened himself to the ether. He doubted he'd notice anything Lyra missed, but you never could say for sure. A few seconds later he was forced to agree. "Me either. In fact, I sense nothing at all, living or demonic. If there's more than a few bugs and rats in the castle I'd be shocked. Should we sweep it anyway?"

"Of course. We can't very well return and tell everyone it's safe until we're absolutely sure it is. Besides, I need to find my ring."

And so they walked through the ruined keep door. From top to bottom, room by room they searched.

And found nothing.

It was tedious and felt like a waste of effort, but Danny had done this sort of thing many times during his years as a Marine. It was a tense project. Every moment you expected a sniper or IED or heaven knew what. He'd once shot a guy with a machete who was hiding under a cardboard box. The potential for trouble was endless on one of these sweeps.

At last they were forced to admit the enemy had fled. They also found no sign of Lyra's ring. No doubt the demons took it along as a trophy. It seemed to be a popular thing to do.

Back out in the courtyard Danny asked, "What now?"

"If my ring's not here, then the priestess must still have it. I can use a tracking spell to locate it through my connection. Keep watch for a minute." She closed her eyes and the ether swirled around her body before a beam shot out northwest. "I have it. About thirty miles out and moving steadily away. If I had to guess, it looks like they're headed for Demon King Castle."

Danny cocked his head. "Why would she be going to that miserable place? It's empty."

"Not completely empty. I found an open portal to Ardent Lilly's hell. She could send my ring to the one place I have no hope of recovering it. Without the ring, I can't access the hero's sword and armor. When this demon king returns or the next one shows up, that'll be a problem."

"Yeah, and if we want to close the rest of the portals, we can't do it without the sword. Okay, do we give chase or go back to the cathedral to give an update?"

"We give an update. It'll only take a few minutes. With a thirty-mile lead, catching up won't be easy."

Danny grinned. "Nothing has been easy since I arrived on this world. Why should this be any different?"

The pair left the castle grounds and made the short walk back to the cathedral. Inside, Eve, the girls, and all the royals were gathered in the chapel and they all stared at Lyra when she and Danny arrived.

"That was fast," Prince Florian said. "I trust you have good news."

"The castle is empty. We checked every room and found no sign of the demons. As best I can tell they've fled toward Demon King Castle. Ronin and I are going to pursue. Hopefully we'll be able to catch them before they reach Fell Forest."

"It's a shame they escaped," Florian said. "But I am glad to have them out of the city. We'll be relocating to the castle."

Danny hesitated then said, "You might want to wait a couple days, Majesty. All the guards have been compromised by psychic magic. You'll have no protection should something happen."

Florian's good mood withered. "I hadn't considered that. The guards and all the castle staff will need to be cleared before they're allowed to return to work. It would seem, Lady Carre, that we will have to impose on your hospitality for a little longer."

Eve smiled and waved a hand. "It's no imposition. You are all welcome to stay for as long as necessary. The cathedral serves as a sanctuary for all those in need. I'll contact the other temples and we can begin removing any lingering magic."

Florian had the good grace to bow. "We'll be counting on you, High Priestess. Lyra, please return as soon as you can. Having you in the city will make us all feel more secure."

Lyra nodded. "I'll do my best, but I suspect I'll be at least a week."

She turned slightly to face the girls. "You two will be staying with Eve for a little while longer. Behave yourselves and I'll see you when I get back.

Tara and Nora ran over and hugged her. It was a sweet

scene and Danny dearly hoped the little ones could return to something resembling a normal life.

When Lyra broke away, she and Danny headed for the door. They had a long run ahead of them.

○

Nahia waited a full day in her pocket dimension. She wanted to make extra sure the hero was gone. The best thing about her version of the spell was that no one could detect it save when it opened and closed. The bad part was, she couldn't tell what was happening in the real world from inside. If she guessed wrong and the hero was still close enough to sense her presence, then the mission would end in failure and her almost certain death.

As stakes went, they didn't get much higher.

When she was satisfied, the portal swirled open and she stepped out into the royal suite. Fake Richard, her four surviving blackguards, and the final succubus followed her.

"I'd be perfectly happy to never have to do that again," Richard said. "Can you call the servants back? I'm starving."

"It's the middle of the night," Nahia said. "You'll have to endure. I'm going to work on the ritual. This is the kingdom's holy day and I want it ready by midnight."

"Do you think they'll bother praying given all that's happened?" Richard asked. "Plus, isn't there supposed to be a celebration today?"

"That was just a story to keep the populace off their guard. The hero's return and the escape of our prisoners has put an end to all those plans. Let those in the city celebrate if they wish. I couldn't possibly care less. Blackguards, with me. I don't wish to be disturbed."

Her black-armored guardians fell in around her and they

left the suite. The best thing about the ritual was that it focused around ten artifacts, ones she kept hidden in her pocket dimension. Had it been otherwise, the hero would've destroyed it, thus ruining her plans. As long as she had the artifacts, she could complete her task.

On the first floor Nahia had taken over what she thought was some clerk's office. All that interested her was the large desk against the back wall. Once she'd closed the door, she opened her pocket dimension again and pulled out a large black chest. A wave of her hand dispelled the magic keeping it sealed. She opened it and took out ten black stones. Crimson runes ran along the sides of each stone. She'd been forced to sacrifice two of them as misdirections, but that was a price she willingly paid. Ten was enough to do what she had to.

She laid the stones out in a neat row and ran her hand over them. They practically crackled with corruption. Several hundred demons along with her own considerable efforts had combined to form these stones. They would act as a focus for the magic. Once she finished charging them it would only be a matter of waiting until midnight and activating the final spell.

It was so delicious that the only person capable of stopping her had left the city on a useless errand.

Nahia nearly laughed but restrained herself. She hadn't won yet. No mistakes could be made at this late juncture. If she made even a small error now, all her work would be for nothing. She shuddered to think how Ardent Lilly would punish her failure. The thought made her shiver with both fear and delight. Like many worshippers of the Lady of Lust, Nahia enjoyed pain almost as much as she did pleasure. They were two sides of the same coin, despite what some prudes liked to claim.

Darkness formed around her hands and she got busy laying in the final ethereal shapes. Nahia lost all track of time as she worked. Every ounce of her concentration was on the ritual. When the final rune was complete, she blew out a long, satisfied breath. It was done. Now she need only wait until the proper moment to trigger the spell.

The now fully prepared stones went back into their case and into her pocket dimension. Task complete, she flung the door open and turned to the nearest blackguard. "What's the hour?"

"Midmorning, Mistress."

She nodded. Good, this was the perfect time to recall her slaves. Should anyone have the courage to try and stop her, they would make useful human shields.

Her psychic command went out through the ether. Satisfied that she'd made the best preparations she could, Nahia strode down the hall toward the stairs to the second floor. Now all she had to do was wait.

As soon as Lyra and Daniel set out on their hunt, Eve went to the nearest temple, that of the Goddess, Lady of Healing. Their temple was a beautiful white stone building with a single floor which sprawled over a full city block. The chapel was small as the majority of the space was taken up by a hospital. Everyone was welcome and the priests would heal you for free. Those who were able to, offered a donation, sometimes coin and just as often food or even a handmade trinket. Every offering was accepted with the same warmth and gratitude.

Though Adonael was worshipped as the leading archangel in the kingdom due to her efforts to save them from the Reaper's wrath, it wasn't hard to understand why the Goddess was the most beloved.

The temple doors were always unlocked so she went right in. A small entry hall led to the chapel. The priestess on duty, a woman about twice Eve's age dressed in a white robe with a red cross on the chest, smiled as she approached.

"Welcome, Eve. How can the House of Healing be of help to the Crystal Cathedral?"

Eve debated asking for the high priestess, but if this was going to work, she'd have to tell everyone what was happening at some point. Might as well start now.

And so she laid it all out. When she finished Eve added, "The only way we're going to be able to help everyone is if all the temples work together. Since you have the largest space, I was hoping we could bring everyone here."

The priestess was staring at her, mouth slightly agape. A perfectly reasonable reaction to Eve's story. It was one thing when this sort of event happened in a village in the hinterlands, but quite another when it happened in the capital.

"Are you quite alright?" Eve asked.

"Yes, yes, I'm fine. It's just a shock. We only have six patients at the moment, so there's plenty of room to work. We can set it up like a clinic. I'll speak to the high priestess and start getting things set up."

"Excellent. I'll go to Branik's temple next. Once we're finished gathering the healers, we'll need to canvas the city for anyone who worked at the castle. I have to assume they're all compromised."

"Isn't there a list of workers?" the priestess asked.

"If there is, I have no idea where to find it or who might know its contents. Given our options, I think it'll be simpler to go door to door."

The priestess had no other questions so they parted

company. It took Eve most of the morning to rally the other temples, but around midmorning they were all gathered at the House of Healing. Branik's temple had sent warriors as well as priests in case they ran into trouble. Eve found herself walking down the street beside a nervous fellow of about twenty years. He kept darting looks at her as if she were going to gobble him up at any moment.

"You can relax," she said. "I'm not going to yell at you."

He offered a hesitant smile. "No, ma'am, I'm sure you won't. I just don't want to make a mistake. You are basically the most important person in the city."

Eve shook her head. "All the people are important. That's why we're out here trying to find ones we can help."

They arrived at the first apartment building in their assigned neighborhood. Before they could approach the door, four people emerged, three dressed like servants and the third wearing a mail shirt covered with a red-and-gold tabard. They all ignored Eve and strode with steady, determined steps toward the castle.

"Excuse me!" Eve waved at them, but they continued to ignore her.

She narrowed her eyes and focused on the ether. She wasn't as good at this sort of thing as Lady Shael, but even with her limited skills, Eve could see the psychic magic in their heads was glowing. Someone had activated the control spell. What Eve couldn't figure out was who had done it. The castle was supposed to be empty. The enemy priestess was too far away to affect these people.

"What should we do?" her guard asked. "I can attempt to restrain one of them if you wish."

"No. They're liable to fight back and I don't want anyone getting hurt. The whole idea is to help them. Let's follow along and see what happens."

So they did. It was like the slowest parade in the city's history. And an ever growing one. As they passed through each neighborhood, more people, again a mix of servants and guards, joined the line as they trudged toward the castle. By the time they reached the road that led to the castle itself Eve was pretty confident the entirety of the garrison and staff had joined the group.

Assuming someone had snuck back after Daniel and Lady Shael cleared the castle—and she could see no other possibility—Eve figured it was best not to get any closer. The last thing she wanted was to end up having to fight these unfortunate people.

"Let's go back," Eve said. "It looks like we won't be healing anyone today after all."

The two of them turned and hurried back to the temple district. Eve dearly hoped someone would have an idea about what to do since she certainly didn't.

CHAPTER 9

I n the end, no one else had a viable idea about what to do for the enchanted people. A pair of warriors had gone to observe the castle at Eve's request and they reported that the guards were performing their duties as if nothing was wrong with them. Eve shivered. Mind control magic terrified her. The victims probably had no idea anything was wrong.

With no other options, she'd gone through with the Holy Day rituals. The cathedral had been packed with people grateful for the end of the war and eager to offer their gratitude to Adonael. As she stood behind the altar, Eve wanted to scream that the war wasn't over. That they had been manipulated and deceived. The only reason she didn't was her fear people would think she'd lost her mind.

Eve needed to retain her authority if she was to have any hope of leading the people through whatever new danger was about to appear. And she had no doubt something bad was going to happen.

At last the day was finally over. She shook the last parishioner's hand and closed the cathedral door behind him.

What a day. Her whole body ached and she wanted a hot bath in the worst way. A little healing magic would cleanse the pain, but she hated using her magic for such minor discomforts; it could easily become a crutch.

"Eve?"

She turned to find Prince Florian sitting in one of the pews looking at her. The young man wore the gloomiest expression she'd ever seen. He'd stayed in the back rooms out of sight during the ceremony along with the rest of the royals. Tara and Nora were playing in her room. The two girls had pretty much taken it over at this point, not that Eve minded.

"Majesty, what's on your mind?"

"Is Villipan doomed? Is it my destiny to be king of a dead nation?"

Eve wanted to reassure him, almost as much as she wanted someone to reassure her. But the truth was she had no idea what the future held.

"I don't know, Majesty. We will all do our best to ensure the people's survival, but we can't control what our enemies do. Given our limited number of soldiers, I doubt it would be possible to retake the castle and defeat both the demons and those under their control. I fear our only option is to wait until Lady Shael returns. With her strength, we should be able to seize victory."

"I shouldn't speak ill of the dead," Florian said. "But I find I wish Father hadn't ordered the hero killed. He was a bit of a rough character and lacked the proper respect for his betters, but I would dearly love to have him with us right now."

Eve bit her lip. Should she tell him about Daniel? No, it wasn't her secret to share.

"I take it from your lack of reaction that you're aware of Father's treachery."

"I am. Lady Shael informed me when I relayed the news of the demon king's survival. Treating Adonael's chosen champion so cruelly after he fought to save us all disgusts me. I understand the king has to do what he thinks best for the country, but I cannot, I will not, accept that murdering the hero was right."

"It certainly didn't turn out well in the end." Florian brushed his hair back and offered a humorless smile. "Pity I'm stuck cleaning up his mess. But I suppose that's the fate of all princes to one extent or another."

As far as Eve was aware, all Florian had done to clean up the mess, as he called it, was mope around the cathedral. Though in his defense, he couldn't do much else. At the end of the day, a king without an army was just a man. And in this case a young and inexperienced man.

"There's nothing to be done for the moment. You should rest. You'll need all your strength when the time comes."

Florian stood and let out a bitter snort. "When the time comes to do what? Walk back to the castle after others have secured it for me? I believe I could manage that much right now. But I'll trouble you no more. I appreciate you indulging my pessimism. Good evening."

The prince walked back the way he'd come, leaving Eve alone. With nothing better to do, she went to the altar and bowed her head. "Please, Adonael, tell me what I should do. The situation looks so bleak, but there must be a way to turn it around."

Minutes passed, but the archangel remained silent. That drew a sigh from Eve. Usually the forces of Heaven preferred to let the mortal realm handle their own problems. It was part of respecting their freewill, or so Eve had been taught.

Sometimes she wondered if maybe Heaven had no better idea how to fix their problems than they did.

When it became clear that her prayers were not going to be answered, Eve straightened and headed for her room. Despite the circumstances, playing with the girls always cheered her up. They had such bright personalities and they'd already mostly recovered from their respective ordeals.

When she slipped inside, she swallowed a sigh. Both of them were in bed, sound asleep. Well, so much for that plan. Instead she settled into the soft leather chair she'd pressed into service as her bed and pulled her blanket over her.

Hopefully things would look better in the morning.

E ve came awake with a scream stuck in her throat. She couldn't remember the nightmare, only the overwhelming fear. A moment later the girls sat up and wailed.

She conjured a light and hurried over. "It's okay, it was just a bad dream."

They clung to her, bodies trembling. Eve stroked their hair and whispered nonsense to try and calm them. Slowly they relaxed and as they did, she did as well. What didn't go away was a sort of psychic chill and powerful sense of foreboding. She didn't know what was going on, but it couldn't be good.

"Are you two okay now? I need to go check on something."

"We're okay," Nora said. "We'll be brave like Daniel said."

Tara nodded but didn't speak.

Eve hated to leave them alone, but she had to see what was going on. Halfway to the chapel she ran into Sister Rose.

"Do you feel it as well?" Eve asked.

The older priestess nodded. "I've never experienced anything like this. Do you know what's causing it?"

"No, but I mean to find out."

Eve hurried through the halls, into the chapel, and outside. The sense of wrongness hit her even harder without the cathedral's protection. It was pitch black, the night of the new moon, and she couldn't see a thing. Looking up at the clear night's sky she could barely make out black lines, mostly based on where they blocked familiar stars.

Squinting, she traced the lines back to their source. It came as no surprise that it was the castle. It looked like they ran from there to the wall. When she counted, she came up with ten lines spaced out around the city.

"What does it mean?" Sister Rose asked.

Eve wasn't sure if it was directed at her or Adonael, but she said, "I don't know, but I fear we'll all find out in the morning."

They returned to the cathedral and Eve instantly felt better. Adonael's protection did wonders to stave off the effects of whatever was going on outside. In the chapel the entire Villipan royal family was waiting. They all had haunted looks in their eyes. Oddly, none of the Forte clan had come out of their rooms.

"What's going on now?" Florian asked.

Eve described what they saw. "As to what it means, I can't say yet. Dawn's light will reveal much."

Princess Clara ran trembling fingers through her hair, which came out in clumps. She didn't seem to be aware she was doing it. Eve's eyes widened when Princess Claudette put an arm around her sister and pulled her close. It was the first act of genuine kindness Eve had ever seen the young woman perform. Perhaps Florian wasn't the only one changed for the better by this crisis.

No one said anything about going back to sleep, but Eve returned to her room anyway. She didn't like leaving the girls alone with everything that was happening. They were awake when she arrived, the blanket pulled up to their eyes as if they were hiding from the darkness. Eve wished she could hide from it as well, but as high priestess, it was her duty to confront evil, not hide from it.

With nothing better to do until morning, she sat on the edge of the bed and read the girls a story from one of her books. She lost herself in the rousing tale of a hero defeating an evil dragon. It was a very simple story with a happy ending. So much less complicated than real life. If only defeating the top bad guy was enough to make things right in reality.

When she finished, she closed the book only to find the girls had fallen back asleep. Ah, the resilience of youth. She'd noticed it several times and wished she shared their mental strength. The idea of falling back asleep, knowing what was running through the sky right now, made her shudder. Instead she slipped silently over to her chair and sat down.

After a long night of waiting, Eve snuck out of her room and returned to the chapel. Everyone was still there and the Forte clan had emerged to join them. After a brief good morning, she went right for the door. Everyone fell in behind her.

Outside, the black lines had been transformed into a dark dome. The sky was visible but dim. Citizens were standing in the street staring up at it. They wore bemused expressions that were no doubt mirrored on Eve's own face.

Out of curiosity, she sent a stream of pure ether up into

the dome. The energy hit and bounced off without making an impression. As expected it was a powerful spell. If it could stop energy, could it also stop objects? If the city were sealed off, food would soon become an issue. Once that happened, the people would really panic.

The face of a beautiful but cruel woman appeared in the sky over the castle. "People of Villipan City," the woman's voice thundered at near-painful volume. "You are all my prisoners. Behave and you will be allowed to go about your normal lives. Troublemakers will be sacrificed to Ardent Lilly. These are your only options: obey or die."

And with that grim announcement, the face vanished.

All around Eve, the royals were staring with stunned disbelief. And she didn't blame them. Eve could hardly believe what was happening herself. But they'd all better get their act together if the city was going to survive.

CHAPTER 10

Danny was thoroughly sick of running. He and Lyra had been running more or less nonstop, their strength maintained by magic, for two days. He had no mental energy to think about anything else; just putting one foot in front of the other took everything he could muster. They had to be sixty miles north of the city by now. Covering this much distance so quickly would've killed a horse. At the moment they were running down a road cut through an evergreen forest. The scent of spruce filled the air, reminding Danny of an air freshener.

"We're getting close," Lyra said. "I can sense my ring about a mile ahead and it's stopped moving."

"She setting a trap?" Danny asked. "If so, we'd best approach more cautiously."

"I don't know what she's doing, but you're right about not walking into anything unprepared. When we're half a mile out, we'll slow to a walk. Do you have enough strength to fight?"

"Depends on what we have to fight. If there's nothing

tougher than a priestess, I'm fine. If a small army of demons is with her, that might be a problem."

"Given the amount of corruption I'm sensing, we won't find an army waiting. In fact, as far as I can tell, she's on her own."

"That's weirder than having an army. These people always have pawns or thralls or something to fight for them."

"We'll find out soon enough. Slow down, we're getting close."

Danny was only too happy to oblige. His body ached as the magic left it, but not so badly that he couldn't move or fight. Lyra drew her sword and Danny grabbed the ethersword from storage. They strode on at a steady pace. Lyra's brow was furrowed as she concentrated. Not wanting to be taken unaware, Danny focused on their surroundings. He found no signs of life large enough to be dangerous and no concentrations of corruption.

But there was something strange in the air. He'd never sensed anything like it. Whatever it was didn't feel threatening exactly, just strange in a way that set his teeth on edge. Danny wanted to ask Lyra about it but feared distracting her.

Twenty yards ahead they spotted a body lying at the edge of the road. The black dress made him think it had to be the priestess, but why was she lying on the ground?

"I'll go straight in. You keep alert for any tricks."

"Okay." Danny lit the ethersword and prepared himself for a fight.

He needn't have bothered. Nothing attacked them and the priestess herself just stared at Lyra, a little smirk twisting her full red lips.

When Lyra stood over her, sword at her throat, she frowned. "You're not the one who captured me. Where is she?"

"Still in the castle. You fools have lost. Can you not feel it? My mistress has activated the ritual. Villipan City now belongs to Ardent Lilly."

"Don't lie to me." Lyra flicked her sword, opening a cut on the woman's face. She just smirked wider. "We searched the castle. No one was around."

"Do you imagine you're the only one capable of using a pocket dimension? They hid while you searched, only emerging after you were far from the city chasing me."

"So you were, what, a decoy?" Lyra asked. "Your mistress sent you off to die knowing we'd follow?"

The priestess nodded. "She's very clever. Nearly as clever as the demon king herself. The other demon lords were fools to send those with power but no wit. Ardent Lilly learned from their mistakes. This world will be ours."

Lyra's sword lashed out, sending the priestess's head flying. She patted the body down and claimed her ring.

"What sort of ritual do you think could let them control the entire city?" Danny asked.

"I can't imagine, but we need to hurry back and put an end to it." Lyra's face was set in a grim scowl. "I thought the girls would be safe in the city, but it seems I left them in the worst possible place."

"It's not like we could've brought them with us. Eve will take care of Tara and Nora." Danny felt weird trying to comfort the woman that murdered him, but it seemed like the right thing to do. He justified it to himself by thinking of her more as his employer.

They turned back the way they'd come and started running again. They made ten miles before night fell.

"We need to stop and sleep," Danny said. "If we're too exhausted to do anything when we arrive, there's no point."

"I can't sleep knowing the girls are trapped. We have to keep moving."

Danny stopped dead in the road. He'd been going for three and a half days with only a few hours' rest, sustained by ether and willpower. He was at the end of his string. "I'm exhausted and so are you. Sleep or just rest, I don't care, but I'm done until morning."

So saying, he found a patch of grass on the side of the road and dropped onto it. Lyra walked over, her scowl never wavering. "You wouldn't be quick to stop if they were your granddaughters."

"Hey! If it wasn't for me, they'd both be in the hands of that priestess and you'd be in a cell or sacrificed. So I don't want to hear any of your guilt-trip bullshit. We're all doing the best we can. Lay down, sit down, or stand there all night glaring at me, I don't care as long as you shut the fuck up and let me sleep."

With that, Danny pulled his bedroll out of storage and settled in. The last thing he did before closing his eyes was conjure the familiar ward around himself. He didn't worry about Lyra attacking him this time. She needed him. But her head was all over the place and he didn't trust her not to miss some threat.

If the spell ended up being a waste he was fine with that. At least it would mean he woke up in the morning.

○

Danny and Lyra stood on a little hill overlooking Villipan City and stared. It was hard to comprehend what he saw. The entire city was sealed inside a dark dome. It wasn't totally opaque. The buildings were all visible though it was like looking through a haze.

Danny wasn't sure what he expected to find when they arrived, but this wasn't it.

"I've got nothing in my memories to suggest something like this is possible," Danny said. "Any ideas what we're looking at?"

"It's a corrupt barrier. I've seen them before, but never on a scale close to this. If anything living tries to pass through it, they'll be rotted down to nothing. Demons, undead, and other creatures of corruption can pass through it without issue."

"So it's basically the opposite of those barriers Eve creates. Do you see the lines running through the sky? What do you want to bet they lead to the other portals?"

"No bet," Lyra said. "They're running to the black stones and we assumed they were connected to the portals. This pretty much proves it."

"The only positive thing I can see in all this is that we don't have to look for hidden stones anymore. Getting into the city, on the other hand, is looking like a serious problem. Any ideas?"

Lyra shook her head, her jaw clenched so tight the muscle looked like a golf ball under her skin. "There's only one way for us to bring it down: shut down the portals feeding energy to the stones."

"Can we do that without Eve?"

"I don't know, but it's not like we have any other options. Even wearing the hero's armor, you wouldn't be able to force your way through."

"Is it a physical barrier as well?" Danny asked. "I mean, if I threw a rock would it bounce off?"

"No, it only destroys organic matter, why?"

"I thought if we got a bit closer, we could try and send a message to Eve, let her know we're working on the problem.

Maybe there's no point, but it might give the people inside hope."

"That's not a bad idea. The message would have to be a short one so it would fit on the smooth side of a stone. Let's see what we can find."

After twenty minutes of searching they found a flat-bottomed rock about the size of Danny's palm. Lyra wrote a brief message with a charcoal stick taken from her storage. Now they just had to move within throwing range. Given how far Danny could throw with his enhanced strength, it shouldn't be too difficult.

They snuck closer, but nothing and no one troubled them. He assumed there weren't so many demons inside that they could send some out to die on a whim.

When they were close enough Danny held out his hand.

Lyra frowned at him. "What?"

"I was going to throw it. Unless you'd prefer to."

"We're not going to literally throw it. You might kill someone. I'll use a spell to carry it over to the cathedral and drop it in front of the door once I'm sure no one's in the way."

Danny shrugged. "That works too I guess."

A moment later the stone flew up, across the city. Lyra's face was twisted in concentration. The magic looked simple, but the beads of sweat that formed on her brow made it clear he was mistaken in his belief.

Five tense minutes passed before she blew out a breath and said, "It's done. What good it'll do is another matter. Let's get out of here."

"Wait, I had an idea. You said the barrier only stops organic matter. What if we used the hero's sword to smash the stones? I could use it like a spear with a thread of ether on the hilt to pull it back."

"Can't hurt to try, but I don't think it'll work." Lyra opened her storage, pulled out the sword, and handed it to him.

They'd ended up not too far from one of the black stones. Danny drew back and hurled the sword with all his might. It was a good toss, but five feet from the barrier the sword slowed before being sent flying away. He pulled it back to his hand, sheathed it, and handed it to Lyra.

"How did you know it wouldn't work?" he asked.

"I didn't, not for sure, but my theory was that the pure mithril and the corrupt barrier would act like magnets with opposite charges. The closer they got, the harder they would repel each other."

"Figures it wouldn't be that easy. Where to first?" Danny asked as they jogged away from the city.

"The nearest portal. If we can't seal it, there's no point visiting the others."

"Right. Do you have a plan B if this doesn't work?"

"We might be able to tunnel under the barrier, assuming it's a dome and not a sphere. We'd need to go down twenty feet minimum to get under the wall. Even with magic that'll take a lot of time."

"Can't we send an ethereal probe to confirm the barrier doesn't extend that far before we start digging?"

"Maybe. It's not something I've ever tried before. In any case, shutting down the portals is our best chance for success, so let's focus on that."

Danny nodded and asked no more questions. In the end, this was Lyra's country, not his. He'd follow her lead the same as always.

CHAPTER 11

Eve sat in her hard chair and tried not to fidget. She and Prince Florian had joined the high priests of the various faiths in the war room of Branik's temple. Everyone was seated around a table covered with a detailed map of Villipan City. There was also a report with estimates of their food supply along with how long it would likely last given the city's population.

The numbers weren't encouraging.

The Sword Lord's followers were the most skilled in combat and everyone agreed that it would be best to let them host the meeting. Eve was happy it wasn't her responsibility. She had her strengths, but running a meeting like this wasn't one of them.

The high priest of Branik, Thomas Saint, a hugely muscled man with a shaved head and stern expression, thumped the table with his fist. "I believe everyone's here. Let's begin. As you can see, the food situation is grim. We've got about a week's worth in the city. After that, people are going to start getting hungry. Analysis of the dome indicates nothing living can pass through it so sneaking out to find help is impossible. We're on our own."

"We can mitigate some of the food shortage with creation magic," said Lydia, the high priestess of the Goddess. "I'm not sure how long our magic can hold out, but it might buy us some time."

Thomas nodded. "Good idea. It will also help keep the people calm if they know the temples have a solution, however imperfect. But it's still only a temporary answer. Long term, our only chance is to find a way to deal with Ardent Lilly's priestess and bring down the dome."

Prince Florian raised a hesitant hand. "Can we not just charge the castle and overwhelm them with numbers? Tens of thousands of people live in the city. Surely no matter how many demons and priests might hold the castle, we can wear them down."

"That may be a last-resort option, Majesty, but you should know that many thousands of people will die if we take the route you suggest. It may be better than starvation, but that will be cold comfort to the dead. You know how well defended the castle is. Even with an overwhelming numbers advantage, we still might fail."

Florian winced but nodded. "If it does come to that, I'll lead the charge. As king, it's my responsibility."

"An honorable sentiment, Majesty," Thomas said. "But let us hope it doesn't come to that."

"Perhaps the adventurers can help," Eve said. "They're as trapped as we are. They should be eager to do what they can. The Wizards' Guild too."

Thomas nodded. "We'll speak to all of them. In fact, I was hoping you and King Florian would handle the discussions. You're the most well-known out of all of us."

"Of course," Florian said. "Anything I can do. Right, Eve?"

Eve was terrible at talking to strangers outside of leading the weekly prayer but she offered a game nod. "I'll do my best."

"Excellent." Thomas's grim expression softened a fraction. "I have every confidence the two of you will accomplish great things. Though I'm less confident that either of the guilds will be able to solve the current crisis. We'll be counting on the other temples to help out where and when they can. Let's plan to meet here in two days at noon."

"Will it be okay if I invite the guild masters to join us?" Eve asked.

"Of course. I should've thought of that. Hopefully they'll see something we missed. Anything else?" When no one spoke Thomas said, "Meeting adjourned."

Eve and Florian left Branik's temple and paused beside the street. "Should we go to the guilds immediately?" Florian asked.

"Let's go back to the cathedral first. I'd like to change into something less formal. The few adventurers I've met tended to dislike anything stuffy."

Florian's lips twisted. "I only have this outfit."

Eve winced. "You look fine, Majesty. It was more my formal robes that I feared making them uncomfortable. I suppose it wouldn't matter since they'll be talking to the new king and the high priestess of Adonael."

"No, no. You're quite right. I was feeling bitter and helpless and I spoke out of turn. How will I ever lead Villipan out of this crisis if I let something as minor as a lack of fresh clothes depress me? It's pathetic."

Eve patted his shoulder. "You're doing the best you can, same as all of us."

Florian smiled. "I generally dislike being patronized, but somehow when you do it I feel reassured. Let's go."

They turned toward the cathedral and set out. It was early afternoon so they should have plenty of time to visit both guilds.

It was only two blocks and soon they were walking up the path to the doors. Eve frowned when she spotted a large stone sitting in front of the entrance. Where had that come from? It wasn't there when they left for the meeting.

She bent to grab it and froze. Something was written on it. The letters were small, but easily read.

"What is it?" Florian asked.

"Lady Shael and Ronin are going to try and find a way to bring the dome down from outside."

"Is there any chance they can succeed?"

"When Lady Shael is involved, there's always a chance, but I think it's best if we do all we can on our own and if they can manage something from the outside, that would be a bonus."

"Quite right. Still, I find myself a bit heartened to know they're working on the problem as well."

"Me too, Majesty," Eve said, meaning it with every fiber of her being. "Me too."

○

After a brief stop at the cathedral to update everyone, Eve and Florian set back out for the Adventurers' Guild. It was a bit longer of a walk since the guild was in a different district. Eve didn't mind. The temperature was perfect and it was nice to move around a bit. The dim sunlight spoiled the otherwise nice day. It reminded her of their bleak situation, but she tried not to think too hard about the many problems they faced. For at least a few minutes she wanted to try and relax.

Her calm walk lasted until they left the noble district. Soon enough they found scores of people outside, staring at the dome. They were muttering to themselves and she saw one person make the sign of the halo over her head. While they seemed confused and nervous, no one was panicking, not yet.

Then someone spotted them. "It's Lady Carre!"

"And Prince Florian," another added.

Eve wasn't surprised by the recognition. She'd considered wearing disguises, but in the end decided if they could reassure people it was best to do so.

"Good afternoon, everyone," Eve said.

The group crowded around them.

"What's going on?" someone asked.

"Who was that woman who spoke earlier?" another asked.

The questions came in, fast and furious, the volume and fear growing with each one. Eve had no time to answer one before someone shouted the next one.

She raised her hands and patted the air. "Please, everyone calm down. I'll tell you what I know, but I can't do it if you're all shouting at the same time."

The voices quieted and then fell silent. Everyone was staring at her which was worse than the questions. She swallowed her nerves and picked one person, a woman not much older than her, to focus on. When she spoke it was like she was talking to only her.

"We've had a bit of unexpected bad luck. Followers of the demon king have infiltrated the city. They're the cause of the dome." Murmurs of concern rippled through the crowd. Eve hastened to continue. "All the temples are working together to find a solution. That will be much easier if you all stay calm and go about your normal life. However, you do need to stay well clear of the dome. We're not yet certain how dangerous it is, but given who made it, you can be sure you don't want to touch it."

When she stopped to catch her breath, people started asking questions again. Eve shook her head. "I've told you all I know. We're trying to figure the rest out. Lady Shael is on the outside trying to find a way to bring the dome down. Everything that can be done is being done. Please, try and stay calm and give us time to sort it out."

"What about the celebration? The king said the war was over."

Before Eve could say anything, Florian spoke. "The creature that spoke to you was not my father. It was a demon or something that took on his form. The king is dead, but I'm doing my best to take his place."

None of the mutters Eve caught after Florian spoke were flattering. The kindest were "lazy" and "stupid." From his scowl, Prince Florian wasn't thrilled with the reaction either. At least he didn't lash out at the people. They were scared and he was an unknown leader. It was only natural that they wouldn't be excited at the prospect.

"We need to continue our investigation," Eve said. "If you could make a path for us we'd appreciate it. Also, offering your prayers to Adonael wouldn't hurt anything either."

A gap opened and several people made the sign of the halo as they passed. When the group was behind them Florian said, "No one believes in me."

"They don't know you, Majesty. It's not like you spent much time interacting with the commoners. Give them time. Once we deal with this crisis, they'll see you as a competent leader and king. You did well not to lose your temper when they spoke ill of you. That was a good start."

Florian winced. "I'm not proud to admit it, but I find my

courage greatly reduced when I lack a squad of knights to protect me. I've studied the sword, but I've never fought someone who wanted to kill me."

"That's nothing to be ashamed of. I'm scared pretty much all the time. The important thing is that we don't let our fear keep us from doing what we must."

Florian smiled. Eve was pretty sure it was the first genuine one she'd seen since she arrived at the cathedral. "I always thought you were too young to be high priestess, but just then you sounded very wise."

Eve's cheeks warmed. "I can't take credit. I was paraphrasing something Daniel told the girls about being brave. I wish I were wiser, smarter, and more experienced, but I'm not. Like you, I'm doing the best I can."

A few blocks later they reached the Adventurers' Guild. There was no one outside today and no shouts emerged from the waiting room inside. She wasn't sure if that was a good thing or a bad thing. In her limited interactions with adventurers, they tended toward loud and rambunctious.

Florian opened the door and Eve went in first. The waiting room was half full of adventurers, all of them looking grave and sullen. A few had tankards near to hand, but no one was drinking. They all stared at Eve, silent and grim.

She tried to smile but it felt strained. Instead she hurried to the reception counter. Two women and a man were on duty and she went to the younger of the two women, a girl not much older than Eve herself.

"I'm sorry, ma'am, but the guild isn't taking requests at the moment due to the current, uh, situation."

"My name is Eve Carre and the gentleman beside me is King Florian. We would very much like to speak with the guild master about the current situation. If you would be so kind as to tell him we're here, we'd be most grateful."

The secretary stared at them like they'd suddenly grown extra heads. "Forgive me, Priestess. I didn't recognize you in such simple robes. Of course I'm sure the guild master will be eager to speak with you. Please wait here a moment."

The girl hurried away, toward the back of the guild.

The older secretary came over, holding a tray with a pitcher and two cups. "May I offer you two a drink? It's only water I'm afraid. If you prefer wine I can fetch some from the bar next door."

"Water's fine, thank you." Eve accepted both cups and handed one to Florian. It tasted cool and fresh, far better than any well water Eve had drunk before. Perhaps there was some magic involved.

Florian didn't touch his. When she caught his eye, she gave the cup a meaningful look. He sighed and took a sip, before favoring her with an "are you satisfied now?" look. It seemed plenty of the old Florian remained. That was a pity. At least he had his worst instincts mostly under control.

No one approached or tried to speak to them. Instead, the gathered adventurers kept darting looks their way as if they were trying to convince themselves they were who they were and not hallucinations.

It was a considerable relief when the first secretary returned and said, "The guild master is waiting for you in his office. I'll show you the way."

They set their drinks on the counter and followed the young woman through a side door. A short hallway a few yards long led to a closed door. She knocked and pushed it open before moving aside to let them pass.

Inside, the office had a lot more personality than the undecorated hall. A suit of armor on a wooden stand stood in one corner, and a bookcase filled with odds and ends but no books covered most of the left-hand wall. Behind the office's desk waited a gray-bearded man in a tan tunic and trousers. Eve guessed his age at around sixty.

"Majesty, High Priestess, please, take a seat." He waved them into the chairs in front of the desk and waited for them to sit. When they had he settled into his own chair. "My name is Felix, guild master of the Villipan City branch of the Adventurers' Guild. How can we be of service?"

Eve glanced at Florian, but he made no effort to speak. Looked like it was up to her. "We're looking for help in dealing with the dome of corruption covering the city. We have very limited manpower so adventurers seemed like the best place to find help."

"Can you tell me more about the dome?" Felix asked.

"I wish I could, but I don't understand how it works or came to be myself. Our next stop is the Wizards' Guild. Hopefully someone will be able to help us figure it out."

"How about the woman whose head appeared in the sky?"

"There I can be of more help. The woman's a priestess of Ardent Lilly. She and her followers infiltrated the city and took control of the castle and all the knights, guards, and servants. We're fairly sure the city watch hasn't been taken over, but I need to confirm each individual."

"That explains your manpower issue. What about the king? He indicated that the war was over and things were going back to normal."

"My father is dead," Florian said. "Whatever the thing that's wearing his form might be, it's not him. Anything it told you about the crisis being over is a lie. We are still in it up to our necks."

"My condolences, Majesty," Felix said. "That certainly explains a lot. The problem is, I can't order the members to help you. That's not the way the guild works. We're only middlemen for the members and clients. If you wish to post a job, I'll waive the guild's fee, but that's about all I can promise."

"Fair enough," Eve said. "When we have a specific request, we'll return and post it. Feel free to tell everyone about the fake king and the dangers we face. There's no point keeping it a secret and the more people who know about the fraud, the better."

"I'll do that. And good luck. If I were a younger man, I'd volunteer to help you for free. Might be some of the others will too, but most people don't become adventurers to risk their lives for free."

"Considering they're trapped in a city with a bunch of demon worshippers and a limited food supply," Florian said. "Doing something for free might be the least-risky option. But it's their choice. Anyone that wants to help should go to the temple of Branik. One of the priests will find something for them to do."

Eve and Florian stood and Eve said, "Thank you for your time. Good afternoon."

They left his office and retraced their steps to the waiting room. As soon as they arrived, a group of half a dozen heavily armed and armored adventurers headed their way. Eve swallowed hard but reminded herself that these people weren't evil.

"Can we help you?" Eve asked.

"We want to know what's going on," said the biggest man, a near-seven-foot-tall bruiser that was nearly as big as an ogre.

Eve repeated everything she'd told the guild master. "Anyone who wants to help would be most welcome. I do recommend staying well away from the barrier as touching it, or worse, trying to force your way through, would be unhealthy."

There was some muttering and a lot of grim faces.

"So none of it was true?" the big man asked. "And now we're stuck here?"

"We're all in the same boat. If it comes to a battle, your help would be most welcome," Eve said. "If there's anything you can do for the ordinary citizens, it would be helpful."

The big man's expression was bitter. "A lot of folks don't think much of adventurers. Unless they need guards or a monster killed or cheap labor they just want us out of sight."

"Most people don't think much of nobles either," Florian said. "The trick is to not take it personally."

"Is that what you do, Majesty?" he asked.

"Not yet, but I'm working on it." Florian said it with such a deadpan delivery that the adventurers burst out laughing.

"You're alright, Majesty," the big man said. "When the time comes, if you need fighters, come find us. My name's Leo, elite adventurer and leader of the Golden Claws."

Florian nodded. "Much appreciated, gentlemen."

Calling them gentlemen got everyone laughing again. Eve and Florian hastened to take their leave.

Outside, the prince said, "I wasn't trying to be funny. Father used to say a ruler would always be disliked. Whenever anything goes wrong it's your fault, even if it isn't. You just had to do what was best for the kingdom even if you were hated for it."

"Good advice," Eve said. She didn't add that it also sounded like a good way to justify doing what you wanted even if everyone thought it was a bad idea, like having the hero killed. "Shall we head to the Wizards' Guild?"

Florian nodded. "Hopefully they'll be of more help."

Eve hoped so too but refused to get too optimistic.

CHAPTER 12

The Wizards' Guild was only a ten-minute walk from the Adventurers' Guild. Unfortunately, more people had come out and the trip ended up taking most of an hour as Eve and Florian had to keep stopping and reassuring frightened people that things were under control and they were doing all they could to bring the dome down.

Eve wasn't sure things were under control, but they were doing all they could. Pointing out the former wouldn't do anyone any good, so she did her best to stay upbeat. That was no mean feat, considering. Prince Florian wasn't much help either. He mostly kept quiet or gave answers so brief they were useless. Eve wanted to give him the benefit of the doubt and think he was just overwhelmed, but she could use more help.

When they finally stood in front of the guild, she let out a long sigh of relief.

"This is the Wizards' Guild?" Florian asked. "I expected something a bit grander."

He was right about the building not being impressive. In

fact, it looked like pretty much every other building in the neighborhood: two stories and made of stone with a tile roof. It couldn't be more than a couple thousand square feet. The front door had a heavy bronze knocker and the top-floor windows were cloudy-looking cheap glass. Eve had visited the place once before, right after she was chosen by Adonael, and even then she hadn't been impressed. The building hadn't improved over time.

"Is this your first visit?" Eve asked.

Florian nodded. "The guild master visited the castle once a year to make a report to Father, but I never had to attend. Are you certain we're not wasting our time?"

Eve shrugged. "Can you think of something more productive for us to do?"

"Good point. Shall we knock?"

Eve tried the door pull first and found it locked. Looked like knocking was their only option. She hammered the heavy knocker down three times then took a step back.

Minutes passed and Eve was starting to think they were going to be ignored. She was about to suggest leaving when someone inside unbarred the door and pulled it open. A young man peered at them through squinted eyes. He wore a robe that was either off-white or dirty. Eve put his age at twenty-five and that might've been generous. She assumed it was an apprentice assigned to the door.

After staring at them for half a minute he asked, "Can I help you?"

"We'd like to talk to the guild master, please," Eve said. "I'm Eve Carre from Adonael's cathedral and this is King Florian."

His squinty eyes popped open wide. "Majesty, High Priestess, I wasn't expecting to find such important people outside my door. My name is Guy Soyer and I can talk with you right now. Please come in."

He stepped aside and ushered them into a dusty stone entry hall. The door shut with a thunk and he threw the bar back in place. Eve tried her best to ignore the cobwebs in the corners of the room. A dark hall led deeper into the guild. Given the state of the entry, she wasn't sure she wanted to see any more of it.

"My office is in the back." A little ball of light appeared over his head. "Follow me."

"You're not the guild master," Florian said in an incredulous tone. "I saw him at the castle once. He had to be three times your age."

"Ah, yes, that would've been Master Magrave. We lost him around six months ago, just before the hero was summoned. And he was so looking forward to meeting the hero too. Life is full of disappointments, I suppose. I was his second-in-command and when he died I got the job."

"Wasn't there someone with more experience?" Eve asked.

"You shouldn't judge a person's ability by their age," Guy said, sounding hurt. "I would think a high priestess your age would understand even if no one else did. Then again, when you have an archangel to vouch for your ability I suppose it makes a difference."

Eve winced and was forced to admit he was right. Even with Adonael's blessing, people frequently underestimated and disparaged her. She was embarrassed to have done the exact same thing to someone else.

They proceeded down a hallway and passed several closed doors. When Eve concentrated, she couldn't sense any other people. She also saw nothing in the guild master's mind to indicate it had been tampered with. That was a relief.

"We don't have many members in any case," Guy said. "The king's advisor and I are the only true wizards who call the city home."

"That can't be right," Florian said. "There are arcane knights and surely some of the adventurers can use magic."

"Of course there are." He stopped and pushed the last door at the end of the hall open. "But they aren't true wizards. Most people just want to learn how to make themselves strong and blow things up. They use magic like a warrior wields a sword. They have no interest in research or truly understanding magical theory. That lack of curiosity will keep them from becoming what we call true wizards."

He went through the door, sending the light up to the ceiling. The modest space was remarkably tidy compared to the rest of the guild. A small desk and some chairs took up most of the space, with a narrow bookcase in the corner being the only other piece of furniture.

Guy sat behind his desk and Eve and Florian took the chairs opposite him. "So, I assume you're here about the corruption barrier surrounding the city."

"You mean the black dome?" Eve asked.

"Yes, corruption barrier is its technical name. It has a variety of forms—wall of corruption, for example. Though I've never read about anything on this scale before. If it hadn't been created by demon worshippers and I wasn't inside it, I'd find the technique awe-inspiring. Unfortunately, my curiosity is insufficient to overcome my desire not to be trapped."

"Sounds like you know all about this thing," Florian said. "Anything you can tell us about how to bring it down?"

"There are several options. The simplest is to kill the

caster. Their will is necessary to maintain the magic. Overwhelming it with a larger quantity of holy energy would also work, though given the scale of what we're talking about, you'd have to open a portal to Heaven in order to summon enough power."

Both men looked at Eve but she shook her head. "Not a chance. I could open one for the instant it takes an angel to pass through, but opening one big enough and holding it open long enough to overwhelm this much corruption is impossible for any one person."

"I wasn't really optimistic," Guy said. "Finally, it may be possible to dismantle the spell. I need to examine the barrier more closely to say for sure. I was reluctant to approach on my own as I don't know the wall guards and, while I am skilled at magical analysis, combat magic is another matter."

"We can arrange for a team of adventurers to protect you," Eve said. "And I'll go along to talk with the guards. They all know me, so it shouldn't be an issue."

Guy nodded. "Excellent. I need to make some preparations. Would midmorning tomorrow be acceptable?"

"That's fine," Eve said. "I'll get the adventurers then stop here. I'm looking forward to working with you."

Guy's smile lit up his formerly gloomy face. "Likewise. I'm quite excited to begin."

They all shook hands before Eve and Florian left the guild. It was dusk and Eve was keen to return to the cathedral. Somehow the night felt darker and not just because of the dome. Understanding that it was the psychic chill from so much corruption did nothing to make her feel better about it.

When they'd gone a block Florian asked, "Do you think he can be of use?"

"He sounded knowledgeable. At this point, Majesty, I

don't think we can afford to be picky about whose help we accept."

"I suppose you're right. Desperate times and all that. I just wish he had a bit more experience." Florian's face twisted into a humorless smile. "I suppose you find it ironic for someone like me to say that."

"Perhaps a little, but it wouldn't hurt anything if we all had more experience. In the end, we're the ones that are here, so we're the ones who have to deal with it. Our wishes to the contrary be damned."

Florian nodded. "Do you ever feel so out of your depth it's like you're in a lake and you're slowly sinking to the bottom?"

"All the time."

"Then how, in heaven's name, do you stay so cheerful?"

"Heaven is exactly how. I have faith that we're on the right side and, if we do our best and don't give up, everything will work out. Call me naïve if you wish, but I prefer my naïveté to bitterness and cynicism."

Florian offered one of his genuine smiles. "It's so easy to tell you're a commoner. Bitterness and cynicism are beaten into nobles by the time we can talk. I envy your optimism."

Eve knew what people liked to say about the nobility, but hearing Florian just say it outright was a bit of a shock. It also explained a lot about some of Villipan's problems. Not that she had time to worry about societal problems at the moment. The big dome of darkness was a considerably bigger concern.

CHAPTER 13

Around midmorning the day after Eve's initial meeting with Guy, the wizards' guild master, she, along with the adventurers that called themselves the Golden Claws, were on their way to collect the youthful wizard and escort him to the wall. Leo, the group's leader, had been as good as his word, offering to help her for free as soon as she walked into the Adventurers' Guild. Despite his intimidating size and appearance, Leo struck her as a good sort of guy.

Walking down the street surrounded by six heavily armed men wearing armor was a completely different experience from when it was just her and Florian. No one called out to them and the few people she saw hastened to get back inside. What did they think, that the Golden Claws were going to attack people at random? She couldn't understand it. Maybe the dome was making people more nervous than usual.

She turned to Leo. "Is it always like this?"

He cocked his huge head. "What do you mean?"

"I mean people seeing you and hiding as if you're going to gobble them up if they look at you wrong."

"Oh, well, it's not usually this bad. But we do make people nervous. It's something you get used to as an adventurer. Most people seldom carry more than a belt knife. But look at us, we look like we're on our way to a war. For people who have never seen combat that has to seem strange."

Eve frowned. "So you're okay with it?"

Leo shrugged. "Doesn't matter if I am or not. I can't change how people look at us. The best we can do is complete our contracts and not raise hell. Long as you do that, most folks won't give you a hard time. The guards in Villipan are pretty reasonable too. I traveled a bit outside the Five Kingdoms and some places are real quick to tell you what's what. Do this, don't do that. I've never been kicked out of a town, but you can always tell when you're not wanted. Villipan City is pretty welcoming in comparison."

"Sounds tough," Eve said. Though she was saying it to Leo, she was thinking about Daniel and the troubles he'd face in his new life. Of course, considering what'd happened to him since he was summoned to this world, the troubles of an adventurer wouldn't amount to much.

They reached the Wizards' Guild a minute later and Eve knocked. Guy must've been waiting for them as the door opened only a moment later and he stepped out. He wore a heavy gray robe and had a bulging satchel over his shoulder.

"Morning, Lady Carre. Your timing is excellent. I just finished collecting the final item I'll need to analyze the barrier."

"Great," Eve said. "And no need to be so formal. You can call me Eve. The rather large gentleman beside me is Leo, leader of the Golden Claw adventurer party."

Guy said, "I've heard of you. Your group is the one that

slew a lesser wind drake about four years ago, right? I so wanted to buy a few scales."

"That was a hell of a job," Leo said. "I don't know who started the rumor it was a drake, but it was actually a giant glider lizard. It could use wind magic, but if it had been a drake we would've been in even worse trouble. I lost half of my original team before we killed that damn thing as it was. I'll never hunt another one for as long as I live. The money was fantastic but it's not worth the risk."

Eve was surprised at how well the two men hit it off. She figured the wizard would be more nervous. Not that she didn't appreciate a pleasant surprise.

The group headed for the wall. It wasn't an especially long walk, but Eve wanted to check in with the guards at the gate. If they saw strangers climbing the battlements it might lead to a confrontation she didn't want.

She needn't have worried. When they reached the gate it was abandoned aside from one body lying on the ground in front of the open portcullis. He was only a couple feet from the barrier.

"Where is everyone?" Leo asked.

Eve shook her head. "Maybe they figured that with the dome here, guarding the gate was meaningless."

While they were talking, Guy hurried over to the body. He made a couple of passes over it with his hands then nodded to himself before rejoining them. "Looks like he rather unwisely decided to touch the barrier. All his life force was drained in an instant. As best I can determine it happened yesterday. There's no lingering corruption in his body and, barring direct action from a demon priest or diabolist, no danger of him rising as a thrall or undead. Though if the body lingers too long near such a potent source of corruption, that may change."

"I'll bless him to be on the safe side," Eve said. "And we can bring the body back to the temple district. The priests of Branik might know him or someone that can identify him. I'm sure his family is worried."

She went over, made the sign of the halo above the body, and a moment later a golden glow surrounded it before vanishing again.

"Done," Eve said. "Can you do what you need to down here?"

"I can start here, but at some point I'll need to work my way around the city as I trace the shape of the spell. Until I grasp what we're dealing with, I won't be able to start figuring out a way to unravel it."

That made sense. "Okay, if any of us can do anything to help, just say so. Otherwise we'll keep our distance and watch for trouble."

Guy was already pulling magic thingamajigs out of his satchel, clearly not paying the least attention to Eve. That was fine. She wanted him focused on the problem at hand.

"Do you think there's going to be trouble?" Leo asked.

"I have no idea. If the priestess notices what Guy's doing, she might do something. I don't know how many demons she has at the castle. My best guess is not many and I doubt she'll be anxious to send them out. On the other hand, I can't say what she's capable of, so it would be wise to stay on our guard."

Leo smiled, revealing six missing teeth. "No need to worry—we're always on our guard. It's a habit for adventurers. I've talked to some of the old-timers and even after they retired, it never goes away."

Eve couldn't make up her mind if that was a good thing or a bad thing. It seemed like a hard way to live.

"Um, I didn't offend His Majesty when I spoke to him at

the guild, did I?" Leo asked. "I was talking before I realized exactly who he was then I was too nervous to stop."

"He didn't say anything about it to me," Eve said. "Under the current circumstances a breach of decorum is hardly a big-enough offense to bother about."

Leo relaxed a bit and said nothing more about it.

Despite them keeping a wary eye open, nothing and no one showed up. Guy worked without a sound until noon when he finally blew out a long breath and turned to face them. His expression gave nothing away, though his little frown did make her think maybe it hadn't gone as well as he'd hoped.

"What can you tell me?" Eve asked.

"A fair bit and also less than I'd like. The locus of control is definitely in the city and I'm ninety percent sure it's the priestess. The power source, interestingly, isn't in the city. Somehow she's bringing all that corrupt energy in from elsewhere. I can't home in on the source from down here, but I'm confident I'll manage once I finish mapping the complete spell."

"I'm pretty sure I know where the power is coming from," Eve said. "I was helping Lady Shael seal a number of portals to Ardent Lilly's hell. We had a lot of work left to do when the current crisis broke out. My guess is those portals are the source."

"That would certainly do it. I need to get up on the battlements and begin tracing the spell."

"Let's eat lunch first," Eve said. "You've been working for hours nonstop."

Guy cocked his head. "I do that all the time, it's not a big deal."

"And that's why you're so skinny. I brought sandwiches from the cathedral, enough for everyone, so let's dig in."

They all ate with enthusiasm. No doubt the fact that Sister Rose made it rather than Eve herself had a lot to do with their reaction. Not that she couldn't manage a sandwich, but Eve's cooking skills left a lot to be desired. That's what you got when you spent your life studying magic and religious texts.

When everyone had finished their meal, the group formed up with Eve and Guy in the center. They made the short walk to a set of stone steps built into the wall and climbed up to the battlements. This time Guy didn't take anything out of his satchel. Instead he held his hand over his eyes and peeked through the gaps of two fingers. She'd never seen anyone use that technique before. Curious as she was, Eve didn't want to interrupt.

They followed Guy as he worked his way around the wall. The group covered about a hundred yards an hour. It was certainly one of the more tedious tasks she'd had to perform. On the one hand, the boredom was far from enjoyable, but on the other, nothing had attacked them, so that was good. Eve wished she knew whether the priestess was ignorant of their efforts or if she knew and deemed them no threat.

"What the hell is that?" one of the Golden Claws asked.

"That" turned out to be a black stone floating about four feet above the battlement. It was a perfect match to the one she found when she was on a mission with Daniel and Lady Shael. Looked like their theory about the stones' purpose had been incorrect.

"It's dangerous," Eve said. "There are demons inside of it so make sure you don't touch it."

"I wouldn't touch it for all the gold in the royal treasury," the man assured her.

Guy stopped when he reached the stone and lowered his hand.

"Are you okay?" Eve asked.

"This is the most concentrated source of corruption I've ever encountered. I'm astonished such a thing exists."

Eve explained how the one they found exploded and a bunch of demons showed up. She made sure to downplay Daniel's part in killing them, making it sound like Lady Shael had done most of the fighting.

When she finished, she added, "I assume this is the same as those."

"Most likely," Guy said. "And I have no way of destroying one in any case. They're a part of the barrier and protected by it."

"Do you think you could destroy it if it wasn't part of the barrier?" Eve asked.

"Probably not, but as it is now, the job is impossible. Anyway, I'm going to return to work." Guy put his hand back over his face and started inching along once more.

The Golden Claws kept a watchful eye on the stone, but eventually they left it behind. At dusk they reached a second stone identical to the first. Guy lowered his hand and wiped sweat from his brow.

"That's it, I'm done for today. We can pick up here in the morning. I've got a pretty good idea what the spell's design is going to look like, but I should be able to confirm it by the end of the day tomorrow."

"Can you give me a hint?" Eve asked.

"It's a repeating design that connects each stone and fuses their individual corruption into the barrier. While the scale is impressive, the design isn't terribly complex. If it were only protecting a tower or even a modest castle, I'd say the odds of me finding a way to unravel it were pretty good. But the raw power on display here is too much for me to handle. Assuming, of course, that I don't find a weak spot in the spell. If I do, all bets are off."

Eve swallowed a sigh. That was a less encouraging report than she'd been hoping for. They found a set of steps to the ground, once again unguarded, and made their way back to the Wizards' Guild. They didn't encounter a single person on the street. The silence was creepy and their pace quickened until they were almost jogging.

In the end they reached the guild without issue and Guy said, "Will you come for me at the same time tomorrow?"

"I was hoping earlier since you don't have to collect your gear," Eve said.

Guy shook his head. "Doing all that analysis wore me out. Plus I want to do a bit of research. Midmorning would be perfect."

"If that's what you prefer," Eve said. "See you in the morning."

They parted ways and the Golden Claws escorted her toward the cathedral. As they walked Leo asked, "Pardon my crude language, Eve, but how deep in the shit are we?"

Eve tapped her chin. "About that deep. If we sink any deeper, I'm not sure how we'll climb out."

CHAPTER 14

D anny and Lyra had been running east for two days as they followed the black, flickering line through the sky. The countryside was quiet and the late summer weather beautiful. He noticed a few of the leaves had started to turn. Despite his threats to the contrary, Danny had no intention of walking away now.

Under other, less frantic circumstances, he might have found the journey pleasant. But given the stakes, all he could think about was getting to the portal as soon as possible. Whether they had a chance of closing it was another matter. Since it usually took his and Eve's combined strength to seal a portal, he had serious doubts Lyra could fill in.

But they'd find out soon enough. The edge of Fell Forest was just ahead.

"Is this where you figured the next church would be?" Danny asked.

"No, I assumed it would be further north based on the others. Going by the spacing of the lines, it looks like I overestimated the number of churches by about fifty percent. This is one occasion I'm glad to be wrong."

"Yeah, no kidding. Just having one thing go our way is nice. I don't know about you, but I feel like I've been led around by the nose since I got here."

"I blame myself for much of that. Despite knowing Ardent Lilly had a far different personality than the other demon lords, I acted like she'd use the same plan and try to overwhelm us. That was foolish on my part."

Danny wanted to argue with her—why he felt the desire to reassure the woman was another matter—but in the end she was right. He didn't know enough about the demon lords to say so. It was one of many large gaps in his host body's studies. Of course, the kid was only sixteen when he died, so it wasn't reasonable to expect him to be a sage.

At the edge of the woods Lyra stopped and cocked her head. Danny knew that expression and kept silent.

At last she said, "I sense no demons or monsters, just the powerful corruption of the active portal."

"Wouldn't that be enough to shield anything nearby from detection?"

"Possibly, assuming they were close enough to the portal. At minimum I'm confident we won't run into anything until we reach the church."

"Good to know." Danny opened his storage and pulled out the ethersword. Holding the mithril hilt eliminated the corruption-induced nausea. "You should take the hero's sword. Being an elf-blood, I imagine this is harder on you than me."

"The opposite, actually. The blood of Heaven offers me some protection from corruption. But on the off chance we run into something unpleasant, having the sword out is a good idea." She grabbed it out of her storage and Danny shifted to make sure she couldn't get behind him.

"As I said, I have no intention of killing you again," Lyra said.

"Keeping you in front of me is an instinct now. Try not to take it personally."

Lyra marched into the forest and Danny followed a couple steps behind. As always, Fell Forest was a dark, gloomy place, made more so by the massive amounts of corruption being pumped out by the portal.

They set a quick pace but even so it was well after dark when they reached their destination. Under conjured lights, Danny looked the clearing over. No demons or monsters guarded the area, just as Lyra predicted. There was also no church. What was left of it, mostly broken boards, was scattered around like a kid's building blocks. A pillar of darkness obscured the portal, shooting into the sky before bending toward the capital. He knew the portal had to be in there somewhere. Getting to it, on the other hand, was going to be a problem.

"This is so much worse than finding a bunch of demons," Lyra said. "That pillar is essentially an extension of the dome covering Villipan City. We're no more likely to force our way through here than we would be there. Less likely in fact since we're closer to the source of the corruption."

"So you want to head back and try digging a tunnel?"

Lyra frowned at the portal. "I suppose we should at least try and break through. Maybe if we combine our strength we can force the sword in. That might disrupt the flow of energy."

Danny shrugged and put the ethersword away. "Let's give it a go."

Lyra pressed the sword's tip toward the darkness, stopping about a foot away. Danny put his hands below hers, the heel of his palm on the butt of the sword. Drawing purified ether into his body, Danny pushed for all he was worth.

And accomplished nothing. He could've been pushing on a mountain for all the good he did. The repelling force was too strong.

"This is getting us nowhere," Danny said. "We need another approach."

"Agreed." Lyra sheathed the hero's sword. "Let's go. I'd prefer not to sleep in Fell Forest if I can help it."

"I doubt I could sleep with so much corruption in the air anyway."

They jogged back the way they'd come. The dark, empty forest was creepy, but nothing troubled them. Around dawn they emerged from the tree line. The sun was coloring the sky orange. Hopefully that didn't mean a storm was coming. Danny needed a soaking on top of all his other problems like he needed a hole in the head.

"Back to the city then?" he asked.

Lyra nodded. "I wish we had some way to communicate with Eve beyond throwing a rock at the cathedral."

"Why can't we talk to her at the gate?" Danny asked. "The dome doesn't stop sound, does it?"

Lyra's jaw dropped. "You're right. The demons only control the castle. There shouldn't be a problem meeting her at the gate. Why didn't I think of that?"

"No one can think of everything, not even you. Hell, I didn't think of it until just now. Let's go."

Danny dearly hoped Eve would have better news to offer. Not that he dared get his hopes too high.

CHAPTER 15

Danny and Lyra approached the walls of Villipan City around noon. Two days of nearly nonstop running had left him exhausted and bored. He was almost eager for something to attack him just so he could take his frustration out on it. The only thing he wanted more was about twenty hours of sleep. The way things were looking, he doubted he'd get either.

"Are you just going to drop another message rock through the barrier?" Danny asked.

"Unless you have a better idea," Lyra said.

As Danny thought, he scanned the top of the wall. When he spotted a fair-sized group of people near one of the black stones he frowned and sharpened his vision. They weren't guards, though most of them wore armor. Two were dressed in robes. The man closest to the stone had on dirty white robes while the woman a little ways away from him... Was Eve.

"I have a better idea. Let's shout up at her and tell her to meet us at the nearest gate." Danny pointed at the group.

When Lyra looked, her glowing eyes got brighter and wider at the same time. "What in the world is she doing up there and why is she being guarded by adventurers instead of proper soldiers?"

"Those are both good questions," Danny said. "Shall we go ask her?"

Lyra didn't bother answering, instead striding closer to the group. About twenty yards from the wall she drew a deep breath and ether gathered around her throat. Danny had just enough time to cover his ears.

"Eve!"

He winced, but Eve looked down at them. He waved, considered enhancing his hearing, then thought better of it just in case Lyra felt the need to shout again. He was supposed to be a simple scout after all. Best to let the famously powerful elf-blood handle everything, at least until they were alone.

"Meet us at the eastern gate!" Lyra shouted, albeit at a less-deafening volume.

Eve gave a thumbs-up to show she'd heard. Danny was pretty sure they heard in Forte, but whatever. Hopefully Eve had good news. They could use some.

The pair set out for the eastern gate. It wasn't a long walk, especially considering how much ground they'd covered so far.

"Any guess what they were doing?" Danny asked.

"I assume they were studying the barrier. You noticed the man in the white robe?"

"Yeah, he needs to visit a laundry. His robe looked filthy and that was from a distance. Had to be worse up close."

"Who cares about his robe?" Lyra asked. "The important thing is that he's likely a wizard. I bet they were analyzing the barrier in the hope of finding a weakness."

"What are the odds of success?" Danny asked.

"Lousy, but not zero. Depending on how skilled the wizard is, he might find something people like us, primarily trained in practical uses of magic, missed."

They reached the gate and found it devoid of guards. "I find it very unlikely he'll find something you missed. But I'll be happy to be proven wrong. Where the hell is everyone? Shouldn't the guards still be on duty? None of them had been corrupted when we left."

"Maybe they figured there wasn't much point with the dome covering everything. I'll wager they're looking after their families instead."

Danny understood that. If a man had to choose between protecting his family and faceless strangers, then it was no choice at all.

It took Eve about ten minutes to join them. She approached alone, but the rest of her group was in sight. They were keeping their distance for now and that was fine with Danny. If any slipups were made, the fewer people who heard them, the better.

"Please tell me you have good news," Eve said.

"I wish I could. Unfortunately we found no way to close the portals," Lyra said. "Even our combined strength along with the hero's sword couldn't get through the barrier. Have you had any luck?"

"We've learned a few things. Well, Guy has learned a few things. He's the new wizards' guild master. For the last few days he's been analyzing the barrier spell. All we know for sure right now is that the priestess is the... what did he call it, the locus of control. If we can kill her, the dome goes down. The black stones we found are acting like a focus for the magic."

"So much for the theory that they were some kind of trap

to be sprung when the demon king returns," Danny muttered. "Does anyone else feel we've been dancing to their song since the start of this mess?"

"What do you mean?" Eve asked.

"I mean all the stuff we accomplished feels like nothing but a distraction so she could do—" he waved a disgusted hand at the city "—this."

"Doesn't matter," Lyra said. "The best we could do was deal with the problems in front of us. That there were other problems we were unaware of is unfortunate but not surprising. The dome is our current problem. Let's figure out a way to deal with it."

"If anyone's got a plan, I'm all ears," Danny said.

"Is it okay if I call Guy over?" Eve said. "He might know something useful."

Lyra nodded and Eve waved the wizard over.

"Have you told him anything about me?" Danny asked.

"Only your fake name and that you're working for Lady Shael."

Danny nodded his thanks, relief flooding through him. "I appreciate it."

"You can call me Lyra. I can't remember how many times I've told you that."

"I know and I try to remember." Eve offered a weak smile. "But it feels wrong."

The wizard arrived, ending the awkward conversation. He looked young, only a few years older than Danny had been in his first life, and skinny as a starved rat.

He bowed to Lyra. "An honor to meet you, Lady Shael. I've been a great admirer of yours for years, so getting to talk to you face-to-face is a dream come true."

Danny fought to hide a smile. Lyra had a fan club? Who would've thought?

"I appreciate you stepping in to help out," Lyra said.

"Of course. I have no more desire to be trapped than anyone else. How much has Eve told you about our discoveries so far?"

After a quick recap the two got into an in-depth discussion of the spell involved. Danny tried to follow what they were saying, but his host's memories weren't even close to being up to the challenge. Eventually he zoned out, instead focusing on their surroundings. This would be the perfect time to attack if the enemy was so inclined.

Happily they weren't and after fifteen minutes of magical jabbering, Lyra said, "Then the only way, besides closing all the portals, to destroy the dome is killing the priestess, correct?"

"That's right. Given what I've seen so far, there are no chinks in the spell that we can exploit. The design is very clean and efficient. If the priestess weren't evil, I'd very much like to discuss spell theory with her."

"That's not going to happen." Lyra ground her teeth. "If only we had some way inside! I could deal with that bitch in two minutes."

"I hesitate to mention this," Guy said. "But there may be another possibility. My colleague at the Forte Wizards' Guild was working on an ethereal interruption device. It's a military project designed to open gaps in magical wards. I have no idea whether it could work in this situation, but it might be worth a try, especially given our options."

"You think it'll work on corrupt ether?" Lyra asked.

"I don't see why it wouldn't. Ether is ether, corrupt or pure are just flavors, like red or white wine. It's the only other thing I can think of."

Lyra nodded. "We'll head to Forte immediately."

Danny restrained a groan. More running, just what he didn't want to do.

"I'll continue analyzing the spell. This time with the goal of finding the thinnest spot to activate the device."

"Be careful," Eve said. "King Miles made it sound like Forte was a real mess."

"We will be," Lyra said. "Good luck to all of you."

With that, Lyra turned on her heel and marched away.

Danny shook his head and asked, "What does this magic whatever-it-is look like?"

Guy managed to look sheepish. "It's a black hoop about a foot in diameter. The outside is engraved with runes. When you look at it through the ether, it will appear as a null space."

"I assume it expands since we're not going to fit through something that size."

Guy nodded. "Once you activate the device, your will controls its size. But the bigger it is, the more unstable it becomes."

"Swell. See you later." He jogged off after Lyra. "If you already knew what it looked like, I'm going to feel foolish."

"I didn't, but given its effect I assumed I'd have no trouble identifying the artifact. No harm in asking."

"That's what I figured. We're going to have to pace ourselves on this trip. I don't want to arrive exhausted to a monster-filled ruin."

"I know. Even though it's the closest capital to Villipan, Forte is still a good three weeks away on horseback. That's ten days minimum at our best pace. We can save some time cutting across country, but I'd still estimate two weeks minimum."

"Then I guess we'd better start running."

○

Nahia lay on the king's bed and let her mind drift through the darkness covering the city. She was connected to it. The dome felt like an extension of her soul. Certainly it was every bit as corrupt. Smiling to herself at the analogy, she let her focus drift toward the sliver of pain that pierced her perfect darkness. Adonael's cathedral. That tiny point of light needed to be crushed. Pity she couldn't do it herself. But the rules of the game were the rules of the game. Only her mistress could destroy the cathedral.

What a glorious day that would be. She could imagine the demon king's pleasure when Nahia handed her the city on a silver platter. A shiver ran up her spine when she thought of the rewards, both magical and mundane, that would be hers.

Someone hammering on the door brought the dream to a crashing halt. Grumbling to herself she rolled out of bed and threw her robe over her head. What could whoever it was want? The demons could handle anything short of an all-out assault on the castle.

She yanked the door open and found one of her blackguards waiting. She didn't know any of their names. The men were tools and you didn't worry about the name of your hammer. "What?"

"That same group is studying the dome again today, Mistress."

"And?"

"I thought you'd want to know."

She rubbed the bridge of her nose. "They can study it all they want, I don't care. The barrier is impenetrable. Nothing less than an archangel appearing from Heaven could break through it. Was there anything else?"

"We're getting low on food." That came from Richard, who was sitting on the sofa gnawing on a chicken leg. "The servants mentioned the larder was only a third full."

"That was fast. I assumed they kept a larger supply of food on hand."

"Apparently the castle gets daily deliveries and they stopped a few days ago for obvious reasons. We're going to be getting hungry in the not-too-distant future."

"I'll summon a raiding party," Nahia said. "They can bring back meat at least."

"I like meat," Richard said.

She was pretty sure the fraud liked everything as long as it didn't look like work. Turning back to the still-waiting blackguard she asked, "Did you need something else?"

"No, Mistress." He bowed and hurried away.

When the door closed Richard said, "You should treat such loyal servants more kindly."

"You do know we worship a demon lord, right? Those men all get off on pain and degradation. If I was suddenly nice to them, whatever loyalty they have would soon vanish."

Richard shook his head. "You're all crazy, but the pay's good, so I don't care. I prefer beef by the way, should your raiders come across a cow or two on their hunt. Wait, how will you get food through the barrier without it rotting?"

"Magic. Go back to your meal. I have work to do." Nahia didn't wait for him to speak again, instead she strode right out the door. If keeping her living servants fed was the worst problem she encountered, she would be pleased indeed.

CHAPTER 16

The border between Villipan and Forte was marked by an occasional fort built in the middle of the main trade roads. Danny didn't find the modest wooden building and its flimsy-looking palisade terribly impressive. He was pretty sure he could level it with a single spell if necessary. And unless you had a wagon you could go right around it without issue. That being the case, he didn't know why the powers bothered building it in the first place. The obvious thing missing was soldiers. Danny didn't sense a single life force inside.

"You want to take a look around or just ignore it?" he asked.

"Ignore it," Lyra said, not breaking stride. "Our mission is too important and besides, no one's present to check on."

Danny couldn't argue with that. Since the gate was open, they walked right on through. As they passed through the dirt patch in the center of the courtyard he asked, "What's the point of this place? It would be so simple to avoid."

"It serves as a base for Forte's scouts along with collecting taxes on any cross-border merchant traffic. Since the king-doms are at peace, there's no need for anything more elaborate."

"At peace for the moment you mean. I would think they'd want something sturdier for when that changed."

She shrugged and went out the opposite gate. "No one has unlimited resources. These little forts aren't a priority."

Defending your border seemed like it should be a high priority to Danny, even if your neighbor was on good terms with you. It was one of those things that struck him as a basic duty of the government. Not that he had any say about what the government did. And even if he had a say he didn't care enough to speak up. The fort was the first interesting thing they'd seen since leaving Villipan City. The cookie-cutter villages they passed through were all the same. The main topic of discussion being the upcoming harvest, a subject Danny couldn't get excited about. No one knew anything about what was happening in the capital.

Probably just as well since they didn't want to cause a panic.

"How long until we reach Forte's capital?" Danny asked.

"A couple more days. With any luck we can sneak in, grab the artifact, and be gone before anything nasty realizes we're there."

"Ten gold pieces says we have to fight monsters, demons, and undead before we get our hands on the damn thing."

Lyra shook her head, not looking back. "No bet. Given how rubbish our luck has been, I'll end up owing you even more coin. I—"

She froze and cocked her head. Danny knew that look and immediately sharpened his senses. He sensed the corruption a moment later. Ten distinct sources, none terribly strong. There were also a number of ordinary life forces along with them but he couldn't make an exact count.

Danny took a step toward them but Lyra grabbed his arm. "I know what you're thinking, but we're not here to rescue people. We have to focus on the mission at hand."

"The time it'll take me to deal with those trash-tier demons and set their prisoners free won't interfere with the mission. I'm not going to let them die because you're in a hurry."

Lyra looked like she wanted to argue, not that it would've done any good. At last she said, "Fine, we free them but then they're on their own."

"Agreed. I wasn't looking to babysit them in any case."

Danny took out the ethersword and activated his stealth field before setting off after the demons. He slipped through the field, running along the road like a ghost. He didn't hear Lyra either so she must have activated a stealth field as well. Either that or she was naturally quieter than him. A very real possibility.

Ten minutes later he spotted them. Nine thralls led by one of the lamprey-headed demons he'd come to know and hate. They were herding a group of twenty or so ragged humans to the north. The people were filthy and their clothes torn. The men had been beaten and the women didn't look much better.

Danny charged the mithril hilt with ether then released an enhanced wave of pure holy energy. The white light burned the thralls to ash and stunned the demon.

He charged in, ethersword crackling, and sliced the monster in half. It started to dissolve at once.

Danny put his weapon away and turned to face the people. They were staring at him with wide, nervous eyes.

He didn't want these people to fear him, but given what he'd done, he didn't blame them for being nervous.

Lyra walked up a few seconds later, sword still in its sheath. "Guess you didn't need my help."

Danny shrugged. "Trash tier, like I said. Are you folks okay? If anyone needs healing, speak up. There's a village across the border a couple days east of here. You can take shelter there."

Danny doubted the people of that village would appreciate him sending a bunch of refugees their way, but he didn't know where else they might be safe. Safe being a relative thing at the moment.

"Begging your pardon, sir, but who are you two?" asked one of the men, a middle-aged fellow dressed in slightly fancier rags than the others.

"I'm Ronin and that's Lyra. We're adventurers on our way to Forte's capital."

Someone gasped and one of the women said, "You don't want to go there, sir. It's hell. Every manner of horror you can imagine stalks the streets. They hunt down anyone they see, not that I can imagine many remain after all this time. The demons have moved on to raiding the countryside. It won't be long before nothing human is left in Forte."

"I appreciate the warning, ma'am, but we have a most urgent mission and that's the only place we can complete it. Things seem peaceful for the moment in Villipan. I recommend you turn east and make for the nearest town. Follow the main trade road, you can't miss it. May Adonael guide you safely."

They all lowered their heads and made the halo.

"Heaven bless you, sir," the same woman said. "I feared we were done for. I hope you make it back alive."

Danny smiled. "Me too, ma'am. Best be on your way."

She bowed to him and the group... didn't exactly hurry away, but they did trudge off as fast as their battered bodies would allow.

When they were out of earshot Lyra said, "Sounds worse than King Miles made out. Remarkable considering what he said."

"What are the odds they're building an army of thralls and using the citizens of the Five Kingdoms to do it?"

"I'd say the odds are excellent and after we reclaim Villipan City I'll be looking to hire you to help free those people and destroy whatever they're using to transform everyone."

"Having seen the looks on those poor people's faces, I might help you out for free."

CHAPTER 17

Danny had serious doubts that Forte's capital had ever been beautiful. Everything was built in gray stone in a blocky, boring style. It gave off serious Dragon Empire vibes from back home. By his estimate about half the buildings had been flattened and the rest had suffered some damage. He couldn't make out a ton of detail from his and Lyra's hiding place in the forest half a mile away, so maybe it was better up close.

And maybe pigs would learn to fly.

Of more immediate interest were the lumbering forms of giants stomping through the city. Standing nearly as tall as the royal castle, they were an intimidating sight. Almost as intimidating as the powerful sense of corruption that radiated off the city in waves. It felt nearly as strong as Demon King Castle and stronger if less focused than the dome covering Villipan City.

He'd been expecting it to be bad and wasn't disappointed. Beside him, Lyra's eyes were narrow and her body tense. It looked like she was as concerned as he was about their destination.

"What do you think?" Danny asked.

"I think sneaking in is going to be harder than I first imagined. They've transformed the city into a city of the dead. I've only read about them and I can't believe they did it so quickly. But the truth can't be denied."

The term "city of the dead" meant nothing in particular to Danny. "Would you like to elaborate for those of us who are less well-read?"

"A city of the dead is exactly what it sounds like: a place where only demons and undead can be found. At the heart of the city is a source of corruption that strengthens them and acts like a beacon to summon any others in the vicinity of the city so the master can take control of them. There's a nation in the far north that consists of a number of cities of the dead ruled by different hellpriests. They're constantly at war with each other and the neighboring human lands. Or they were when the book I read was written. A couple hundred years have passed since then so things may have changed. Anyway, sneaking in might not be possible. Anything living entering the city will be detected by the master."

"So we just fight our way through?"

"It may come to that, but I know a spell which allows the living to cloak themselves in an aura of corruption, allowing them to pass as a lesser demon. But there is a risk."

"You mean beyond the fact that I'll be casting a spell I've never heard of for the first time in a life-and-death situation?"

"Yes, beyond that. The aura of corruption opens you to the call of the master. If your will falters for a moment, you risk ending up under their control."

Danny shook his head. "I don't like this plan at all. Too many risks and it could all fall apart way too easily, especially considering how worn out we are. I say we charge in, move fast, cut down anything in our way, and get the hell out."

"Depending on how many thralls they have, even we might end up getting worn down. The risk is huge either way."

"Then why don't we do both?"

Lyra's frown deepened. "What do you mean?"

"You sneak in with the cloak while I cause chaos on the outskirts of the city. The master will be focused on what I'm doing which makes it less likely you'll be noticed. As long as I don't get in too deep, I can always pull back. The city wall has so many holes smashed through it that it won't slow me down."

"That's not a terrible plan. You go in first and when I hear the first explosion I'll sneak in. When I've secured the artifact, I'll send up a flare to signal you to withdraw."

"Got it. Good luck."

"You too." Before he could take a step she asked, "Do you want the hero's sword? I can't use it with the cloak and it might give you a bigger advantage. You can have the armor as well. It's not like they don't know you're still alive."

Danny hesitated but only for a moment. Not wanting to use them was his ego talking. Just because he carried a particular sword and wore some armor didn't mean he was taking on the responsibilities of the hero. And not doing it made him much more vulnerable. Given what they were facing he couldn't let his stupid feelings get in the way of success.

"Alright. It's not like they could miss me in a suit of mithril armor."

Lyra opened her storage and they got busy putting the pieces in place. Danny was tense at first as a flood of bad memories hit him, but when it became clear Lyra had no intention of doing anything he relaxed, a little.

When the last strap was tightened she asked, "How's your movement?"

Danny flexed his arms and bent his knees. "Good. Let's do this."

He took off toward the city at a jog. The armor did make him a fraction stiffer, but the impenetrable metal also made him nearly invulnerable. It was a good trade.

He reached the nearest gap in the wall and leapt through. The street beyond was empty save for rubble from a nearby leveled building. Danny was vaguely aware of the ambient corruption, but with so much mithril around him he suffered no ill effects. It reminded him a bit of walking through fog. It felt a little clammy on your skin, but that was it.

On the downside, so much corruption did hide the location of any demons that might be lurking in the area. He shrugged and started walking, the hero's sword gripped in his right hand. The balance was different than the ether-sword. That weapon's weightless blade made it extremely hilt heavy. The hero's sword was perfectly balanced. Both were excellent in their own way.

He rounded a half-collapsed building and found a giant stomping toward him. The brute stood over twenty feet tall, with massive shoulders and an equally massive gut. Burning red eyes glared down at Danny. The giant seemed to be wondering what this insignificant insect was doing scuttling around in its city.

Then again, Danny was probably giving the stupid thing too much credit.

He charged the blade of the hero's sword with holy energy and launched it at the giant.

The monster raised its arm to shield its face from the explosion of white light.

When it did, Danny sprinted forward and sliced its right foot off at the ankle. A quick spin and a second blow severed the left foot, sending the giant toppling to the ground.

An instant later he reached its neck and hacked its head off, ending its struggles. That was one down and heaven knew how many to go.

Confident that Lyra couldn't have missed his spell, Danny set out to hunt.

◯

When Daniel's holy blast went off, Lyra took a deep breath and summoned the ether around her. That was simple, the tricky bit was corrupting it. For a living person not connected to one of the demon lords, the process took a fair bit more effort. As with all things magical, it came down to picturing what you wanted and having the will to make it a reality. She pictured the pure energy turning black, letting her rage and resentment color her thoughts. Fear for her granddaughters helped as well.

When she started to feel a bit sick, she knew the process was complete. Of course, there was only one way to be sure.

Lyra approached the city, head lowered and moving at a shambling pace. She had to think of herself as a thrall. A difficult task for someone as strong willed as her. But she did it all the same.

Climbing through a gap in the wall, Lyra turned toward

the city center. She'd visited Forte a couple of times over the centuries and unless they'd moved it, that was where she'd find the Wizards' Guild. They had a section of the city set aside for all the guilds, named the Guild District, uncreatively enough.

Ten strides in she felt a powerful tug from the royal castle. It was the master's call. Clenching her jaw, she resisted it. Hopefully he, or more likely she, wouldn't notice the presence of a lowly thrall walking about unleashed.

An explosion shook the air and Lyra almost smiled. Daniel was doing his best to make sure he had everyone's attention.

Keeping her gaze lowered save for the occasional peek to make sure she was headed in the correct direction, Lyra worked her way farther into the city. Having to look at nothing save the broken cobblestones came as a relief. She had no desire to see any more of the ruined city than necessary. The scent of rot and evil—and evil did have a unique scent, though Lyra wasn't sure how to describe it—nearly overwhelmed her. The city of the dead was vile in a different way than Demon King Castle.

A vibration ran through the ground. She paused, started to look up, then caught herself. A second, heavier thud shook the ground. Out of the corner of her eye she caught a glimpse of a calf the size of a tree trunk. The giant was headed toward Daniel and didn't pay her the least attention. When it had gone she blew out a breath and kept moving. She still had a long way to go to reach the guild.

Step after step brought her ever closer to her destination. Twice she caught herself veering off course toward the castle. The master's call was like a constant tug in the wrong direction. Every time her concentration wavered, her course did as well. So far she'd caught herself before she got too far off track, but if she took too long, Lyra feared she might lose herself to the call. She offered a silent thank-you to Adonael that Daniel hadn't come with her. For all his power, his lack of experience might have gotten him in trouble.

After far too long of a walk, Lyra reached the Guild District. It had been smashed as badly as everything else in the city, but some of the buildings were still more or less intact. Hopefully that meant the Wizards' Guild was somewhat secure.

Lyra risked raising her head and took a good look around. There were no demons visible; that was a good sign. Good for her anyway. Daniel was no doubt up to his neck in them. It was a lucky thing he hadn't let his pride keep him from taking the hero's sword and armor. For a moment when she made the offer she feared he might refuse out of some misguided principle, but in the end he'd agreed. Even so, she didn't dare take too long.

Picking up the pace, she made her way down a side street, past the half-collapsed Adventurers' Guild, and around the bend to the Wizards' Guild. As she'd hoped, it was largely undamaged. On the downside, the front door was wide open.

Hand on the hilt of her sword, Lyra slipped through the door. The inside was dark but that proved no issue for her eyes. The entry area, a twenty-by-twenty space with a counter running along the back where potential clients were met, was empty. The counter had been smashed to pieces, making it easy to access the hall that led to the rear of the building.

She hopped over the broken wood, careful not to make a sound. With so much corruption around her, she wouldn't be able to sense any waiting demons. The muscles of her neck and shoulders had begun to ache and she forced herself to relax. Tensing up would only slow her down if she had to fight.

Lyra checked the first floor room by room and found nothing of interest. Not a single book or magical item remained. Someone had thoroughly looted the first floor. If the second floor was in similar condition, they were in trouble.

A set of steps led to the second floor. At the landing she paused and listened. A few seconds of silence was followed by the scuffing of claws on wood. So there was something here. She eased her sword out of its sheath. Now the tricky bit. Since holy energy would burn away her disguise, Lyra would have to use a different, less effective sort of magic. Lightning sparked from her finger and crackled along the length of her blade.

Following the sounds, she tracked what she assumed was a demon around the second floor. A figure stepped out of an open door. It was a handsome man from the waist up and a beast of some sort from the waist down. The incubus spotted her an instant too late.

Lyra sprinted toward it, covering the distance in the blink of an eye. A hard slash opened a deep groove in its chest, but didn't kill it. Cursing her luck she swung again.

The demon dodged and hurled a bolt of darkness at her.

Lyra sliced the spell apart, drew more ether into her body, and attacked again. This time she ran it through the chest and loosed the infused lightning, blowing it to smithereens. Grimacing at the mess she'd made, Lyra sheathed her sword.

She took a single step toward the room the demon had been exploring when the full, powerful regard of the master slammed into her. Fighting with all her will, Lyra tried to resist. Unfortunately, the corrupt ether she'd drawn into her body, while making her strong, also made her more suscep-tible to the master's commands.

One by one her mental barriers were torn down until the master's dark presence reached her mind. When it did, Lyra was helpless to resist.

CHAPTER 18

The third giant Danny cut down landed with a thud and whoosh of wind. The big, lumbering brutes were an intimidating sight, but they were also slow and stupid. He could run circles around them and the hero's sword cut them down to size as easily as a hot knife through snow. He didn't even have to worry about damaging the city since everything was already damaged.

A trio of smaller demons, ugly things with the lower bodies of snakes and the upper bodies of monkeys, came slithering at him. They hurled darts made of black energy. Danny ignored them and they sizzled to nothing against the hero's armor. He had yet to find an enemy here capable of hurting him. It seemed almost unfair, not that he was complaining. When it came to slaying demons, there was no such thing as fair play.

The first snake demon lunged at him.

Danny shifted aside and cut it in half.

The second took advantage of the distraction to attack

from the opposite side. It opened a mouth half as big as its head.

Danny jammed his left fist down its throat then hurled it aside.

The final demon wrapped its coils around him like a python. That turned out to be a poor strategy. Danny channeled holy energy through his armor and burned the thing to ash in seconds. Finally he closed with the second slowly recovering demon and removed its head.

No more enemies presented themselves for execution so he took a moment to catch his breath. He wasn't using a ton of magic, but even so the constant fighting was wearing him down. How long had he been going? Danny wasn't sure, but it felt like a long time.

What was Lyra doing, sightseeing?

On the one hand, Danny didn't want to go too deep into the city, but on the other, he was getting worried. Maybe checking on her wouldn't be the worst idea. He could still keep his distance, but if she was in trouble, maybe he could help.

He glanced around and spotted an intact tower. That would give him a decent vantage point to have a look around. A single leap carried him to the roof of a broken-down store. He kicked off the roof and soared to the top of the tower.

As he'd hoped, it offered a good view of the city. Danny sharpened his vision. Half a dozen more giants were headed his way. They weren't speedy runners, but their long strides ate up the ground in a hurry. It was strange that he felt no real sense of alarm at the sight of them. If you'd told him before he came here that he'd be fighting honest-to-goodness demonic giants, Danny would've been in danger of shitting his pants. Now they were just a few slashes away from becoming rapidly decaying piles of meat.

Ignoring the giants for now, Danny kept looking for Lyra. Plenty of human-sized demons were running around down there. Much like the giants, the majority were headed his way. He tried to put himself in the mind of whoever was running this place. Why would they be sending their troops to certain destruction? He couldn't come up with a good answer other than that they had to do something to stop the intruder and this was the only option available.

He frowned. In a courtyard only a couple blocks from the royal castle Danny spotted a figure that looked fully human. It didn't have beast legs or monstrous features. Though he couldn't see her face, the outfit was right so he assumed it had to be Lyra. What the hell was she doing there? He thought the idea was to stay well away from the castle. And the way she was moving looked wrong too. He'd never seen her move with such ungraceful steps.

Something had to be wrong.

Leaping from roof to roof, Danny hurried toward her. Staying off the ground allowed him to avoid the small fry. One ugly, hairy thing with the legs of a goat sprang up at him. He cut it out of the air without pausing.

A giant placed itself between him and Lyra. Even standing on a roof, Danny had to look up at it.

A club the size of a full-grown tree came crashing down at him.

He leapt again, evading the blow. The building he'd been standing on didn't fare so well. Chunks of rock bounced off his armor like hail. And then he was past it.

Five more long bounds brought him to the courtyard. Lyra was at the far end about to start up the road that led to the castle. A bunch of minor demons came rushing into the courtyard from the opposite end.

It was going to be a race, one he didn't dare lose.

A final jump carried him halfway across the courtyard. As soon as his feet hit the cobblestones, he exploded forward at a dead sprint.

Danny skidded to a stop in front of Lyra. She stared at him with a blank expression, seeming unaware of his presence. In truth he'd seen more awareness on the face of a zombie.

"Hey, snap out of it. You're in the wrong part of town."

She moved to step around him without comment.

The demons were closing in fast. Danny didn't bother examining them closely. They were all just different flavors of the same evil. A wave of his hand conjured a wall of white flames between them. That would buy him a few seconds.

While he was casting, Lyra had moved around him and resumed her trek to the castle.

He scrambled to block her again. "Stop. I don't want to hurt you, but I can't let you go any further. It's for your own good."

Danny might as well have spoken to the shattered rock at his feet for all the reaction he got.

Fine. We'll do it the hard way. He grabbed her shoulder.

Lyra screeched and pulled back. Had the mithril of his gauntlet hurt her? As a living being she shouldn't have been vulnerable. Maybe it had something to do with the cloaking spell she'd mentioned. If she was surrounded by corruption, that might be enough to get a reaction. She must have fallen under the control of whoever was in charge of this dump.

The demons came screaming around the end of the wall of fire.

Shit! He didn't have time to screw around anymore.

He sunk a heavy fist into her gut, doubling her over and dropping her to the ground. With Lyra immobilized, he turned his attention to the approaching demons. There were seven of the lamprey-headed monsters. Barely enough to trouble him now that he had all the hero's gear out.

Going hard with his physical enhancement, he darted in and proceeded to reduce the demons to puddles of sludge. They couldn't lay a claw on his armor much less put a scratch in it.

Safe for the moment, he scooped Lyra up. She moaned when the armor touched her, but he didn't have time to worry about it. He sprinted toward the outer wall, burning anything that got in his way to ash with white-hot flames.

And then he was through and running away from the city. When he'd gone a mile, Danny stopped beside a narrow creek and set Lyra down under a sprawling maple tree.

He took his helmet off and examined her through the ether. Now that they were away from the city, he could see the aura of corruption surrounding her. What he was less certain of was how to remove it without hurting her. A touch of his gauntleted finger drew a hiss of pain. It also burned away some of the corruption.

Maybe there was no painless way to do what he had to. That being the case, fast was probably best. Danny put his helmet back on, lay down beside her, and wrapped his arms around her body.

Lyra started to screech and thrash. Danny winced at the noise but held on tight. When her legs started flailing, he wrapped his own around them. Her volume spiked, drawing a wince. Shame he didn't have an extra set of hands to plug his ears.

There was a time not so long ago when her pain would've pleased him, but that time was past.

After a tense couple of minutes she calmed. The aura of corruption was gone. Soon her breathing was back to normal.

"You can let me go now," Lyra said.

Danny scrambled to put some distance between them. "Sorry, this was the best way I could think of to purify you."

"Don't apologize." She sat up and worked her neck from side to side. "You did what you had to. Given the alternative, I'm grateful you did."

"What happened? I thought you were going to the Wizards' Guild."

"I did. The spell was working perfectly. None of the demons paid me the least attention. Until I found one rummaging around in the guild. It was in the way, but when I went to kill it, I drew more corrupt ether into my body, which opened my mind to the master's awareness. His—I think—will hit me like a ballista bolt. Try as I might, I couldn't fight it off. When he commanded me to come to the castle, I had no choice but to obey. It was a stupid, rookie mistake. I activated my physical enhancements without giving a thought to the fact that I was surrounded by an aura of corruption. If you hadn't been there, I shudder to think what the master might have done with me."

Seeing no reason to comment on her mistake, he asked, "What about the artifact?"

Lyra shook her head. "I saw no sign of it. It looked like the guild had been plundered. The demon I ran into was likely making a final sweep for anything valuable. I fear that if we want the artifact, we'll need to go to the castle and claim it by force."

"You thought that was a bad approach for us," Danny said. "All I've seen are trash-tier demons incapable of slowing me down. I lost track of how many I killed while I was acting as your decoy. Do you think the castle will be that tough of a nut to crack?"

"I don't know and that's why I suggested avoiding it. Now it doesn't look like we have any other choice. Give me a couple more minutes to catch my breath and we'll go."

"Maybe you should wait here. Even purified, your mind might be open to his influence."

Lyra rubbed her eyes. The glowing golden orbs didn't get bloodshot, but she sure looked tired. Hardly surprising given all that they'd done over the past few weeks.

At last she said, "That's not possible and just to be safe I'll activate a psychic barrier. You should too, by the way. Ardent Lilly's followers are too good at mental manipulation to not spend the power maintaining one."

"I keep one active at all times now. No succubus is going to get the better of me again. I can't convince you to stay behind?"

"No. I mean to see this through no matter what."

"So be it. When you're ready, we'll invade the castle." Danny offered a silent prayer to Adonael or any other archangel that the battle wouldn't go as badly as Lyra feared.

CHAPTER 19

D anny and Lyra ended up resting for a full hour before returning to Forte City. As they walked back he kept flicking glances at her. As far as Danny could tell, Lyra was back to normal. Her back was straight and her stride determined. If he hadn't known what just happened to her, he never would've guessed anything was wrong. Hopefully he wouldn't be able to tell when the fighting began either.

A few yards from the shattered wall Lyra caught him looking. "You need to focus on yourself and stop worrying about me. All that matters is getting the artifact. If I die in the process, that's a price I'm willing to pay."

"Easy for you to say. I'm the one that's going to have to tell your granddaughters that I let their grandmother die. Not a conversation I'm eager to have."

"The girls are aware that what I do is dangerous. If the worst happens, they won't blame you."

Danny swallowed a sigh. "I'm not worried about being blamed. I'm worried about breaking their hearts because someone they loved has died. Do they have another person to take care of them?"

Lyra held up her hand. "This is neither the time nor the place to discuss the matter. We need to focus on the mission or one of us really might die."

Danny took that as a no, but she wasn't wrong about the situation. He put his questions aside and drew the hero's sword. Taking the lead, he stepped through a gap in the wall. As far as he could see in every direction there was no sign of demons or giants. He'd expected an uglier welcome.

With a shrug he set out toward the city center. Since they didn't need to sneak around, he made a beeline for the castle. The silence was eerie. He hadn't noticed it with the constant fighting during his first visit, but now, walking down the empty streets, it felt strange.

He imagined the end of the world would feel something like this.

When they reached the castle it became clear where all the defenders had gone. The outer wall was manned by dozens of trash-tier demons. Four giants towered over them all. For anyone else it would've been an intimidating sight. But for Danny it was an annoyance.

"I'll handle this lot," Danny said.

When Lyra didn't argue, he charged forward. His speed increased as his body filled with ether. The armor made it easy to access pure energy and soon he was crackling with it. A powerful leap carried him onto the wall.

A menagerie of ugly swarmed in on him. The hero's sword made quick work of them, each cut slicing one in half. Anything that got close enough to land a blow found it turned aside by his armor. It had to be frustrating for them, not that Danny had any sympathy for demons.

Through a gap in the attackers, he spotted one of the

giants swing its club right at him. Apparently friendly fire wasn't something they worried about.

Danny sprang over the club and a moment later it sent demons and rubble flying in every direction. He landed on the giant's arm and ran right at its head. A hard slice half severed its neck. A back cut finished the job.

Before it could collapse, he jumped again. Using his momentum, he sliced the leg off the next-nearest giant, sending it tumbling to the ground. He ran the length of its body, sword slicing as he went.

He stopped on its chest, charged the sword with holy energy and released it in a wave that rushed out in every direction. When it faded Danny was the only living— assuming that word applied to demons—thing in the court-yard. The giant corpses were already in an accelerated state of decay and he leapt off the one he'd been standing on lest he sink up to his neck in necrotic flesh.

Despite wiping out all the outer guards, there was no reaction from the castle. Danny kept his gaze locked on the closed double doors, but it looked like the person in charge had no intention of sending out a sally force.

"Well done," Lyra said as she walked across the courtyard to join him.

"Thanks. What do you think the point of that was? I'm barely breathing hard."

"Luring us into a false sense of security is the only thing I can think of. Shall we try our luck in the castle itself?"

He nodded and strode toward the closed doors. No one had placed any magical protections around the place that he could sense.

"I don't detect any wards, do you?"

Lyra shook her head. "As far as I can tell, the exterior of the castle is unchanged. Bear in mind it hasn't been that long since the city fell. I'm sure if we'd waited a couple more months, we would've found a different security situation."

Danny hoped she was right, but everything about this setup screamed trap to him. Well, if they thought trapping him was a good idea, he'd be happy to disabuse them of the notion. He shoved the doors but they didn't even rattle in the frame. Someone must've thrown the bar.

Three quick slashes reduced the door to so much kindling. Beyond it, the entry hall was empty and the magical lights hanging from the ceiling gave off a white glow. Tapestries depicting a variety of noble-looking men covered the walls and a thick, filthy carpet of indeterminate color ran down the center of the hall. The corruption was denser here, but Danny hardly noticed it.

He glanced at Lyra. "Are you going to be okay? This place isn't as bad as Demon King Castle, but it's pretty nasty."

"I'll be fine. I told you, the blood of Heaven offers some protection. That said, I'd prefer not to linger."

Right, no screwing around. The sooner they got this done, the happier everyone would be. Still, he couldn't rush lest he walk into a trap.

He set out at a steady walk, the hero's sword raised in ready guard. The castle was as silent as the city and nothing troubled them. Danny paused to check a couple of rooms they passed and found nothing save the remains of smashed furniture. Why the demons bothered to smash tables and chairs was beyond him. Maybe they did it for fun. That would be in character.

He turned down a wide hall with a once-red carpet running down the center. Suits of ordinary armor lined the path. At the end waited another closed door, this one inlaid with a golden crown. If it didn't lead to the throne room, Danny couldn't imagine what was behind it.

As they got closer, faint, soft sounds reached him. They weren't words, more like incoherent moans. They weren't the sort of noises he imagined someone being tortured would make. Sounded more like they were about to interrupt an orgy. Given who was in charge of this place, that wasn't beyond the realm of possibility.

One stride from the door, Lyra froze dead in her tracks. Her entire body was rigid. So much corruption hung in the air that Danny couldn't pick out whatever might be causing her trouble.

"What's wrong?"

"I can't go any further. The master has placed a forbiddance spell on that room. Nothing associated with Heaven can enter. I have enough angelic blood in me to qualify."

"That's fine. You stay here and watch the door. I'll be back as soon as I can."

She took a step back and her muscles relaxed. "Be careful, I don't know how this particular magic might affect you even with the armor."

"I'm as human as it gets," Danny said. "Why would it affect me at all if it's designed to affect angelic creatures?"

"It may not. But since you were summoned from another world, it's possible you might not be considered fully human on this one."

"One way to find out for sure." He stepped forward and kicked the double doors open.

Inside was a scene from either your dreams or nightmares. Insubstantial figures were writhing around in a variety of sexual positions. These spirits were the source of the moans he'd heard earlier. A man in a black robe was seated in the golden throne at the rear of the room. His top was open, revealing a muscular chest and abs. Beside him, a quartet of female demons massaged his shoulders and rubbed his body. On his right index finger he twirled a black hoop. That had to be the artifact Danny was looking for.

He noted and quickly dismissed a trio of rather pathetic-looking thralls on their knees groveling in the priest's general direction. Did he take some sort of twisted pleasure in having creatures he controlled worshipping him? Danny couldn't make any sense of it and stopped trying.

"Welcome, Hero," said the man. "I had hoped the mistress was mistaken when she said you survived. I should've known better, she is a demon lord after all."

"So you're a priest of Ardent Lilly. And here I thought only women served her."

He smiled, revealing perfect, white, slightly elongated teeth. "It would hardly be any fun for the priestesses were there no priests around. Though they do manage to entertain themselves when we're busy."

Danny could well imagine given all he'd seen. "So, shall we get busy trying to kill each other?"

"Why the rush? The show is just getting started." The priest waved at the spirits getting it on all over the throne room. "This is a view into a tiny corner of Ardent Lilly's hell. Glorious, isn't it? When I die, this will be my eternal reward."

"Lucky you. Let's get you there as soon as possible." He took a step closer.

The priest stopped twirling the hoop and took a tight grip on it. "I don't know why you're so eager to claim this little bauble—my mind was cast out of your companion before I found out—but if you come any closer, I'll destroy it."

Danny frowned but didn't move. The hoop looked pretty sturdy, but he couldn't say for sure that was impossible. Since Danny needed it to get into the capital, he was hesitant to take the risk, however slight.

"Okay, but what happens now? If you smash that thing, I'll kill you an instant later. Unless you're hoping for an eternal standoff, something's got to give."

"You're quite right. Here's my proposal. You promise to let us leave the city in peace and I'll give you the artifact. My minions and I are no match for the man who defeated the demon king. And, while I am looking forward to my eternal reward, I'm not eager to claim it yet."

Danny hated it, but the priority for the moment was getting into Villipan City. This asshole was a minor issue. "You'll trust my word, just like that?"

The priest nodded. "I've dealt with you good-guy types before. You have this strange desire to do what you consider the right thing, like keeping a promise, even when it's not in your best interest. I've never understood it, but the truth is, I'd sooner trust you than I would any of my coreligionists."

That was both sad and predictable in equal measure. "Toss it over here and piss off. If you're still in the city by the time I'm done confirming this is indeed the thing I'm looking for, you're dead."

"Your terms are acceptable." The priest flicked his wrist and sent the hoop flying toward Danny.

He looked away long enough to catch it and when he looked back, the throne was empty. Only the still-groveling thralls remained behind. The ghostly adult floor show, on the other hand, was still going strong.

Best to put the thralls out of their misery. As he approached, the creatures turned to look at him. Danny froze. He didn't recognize the woman or the girl, but the man was Miles de Forte, king of Forte. A man Danny had met not long ago in Villipan City.

Something very strange was going on.

Three quick slashes severed the thralls' heads. Danny

sheathed his sword and grabbed Miles's head. Ignoring the demon spirits, he returned to Lyra.

"This is it, right?" Danny asked as he handed her the hoop.

Lyra closed her eyes for a moment then nodded. "Yes, this is the artifact. What are you doing with a severed head?"

"Take a closer look." He held it up for her inspection. "Do you recognize him?"

Lyra stared, her face aghast. "It's King Miles. Give it to me."

Danny handed her the head and Lyra turned it over to examine the back of the skull. He nearly made a crack about searching for a dagger hole, but given her grim expression decided against it.

"What are you looking for?"

"This." She parted the filthy blond hair, showing him a hole half the size of his fist. "He was killed by braineaters. We need to get back. There are monsters in the cathedral with my granddaughters."

"I've never heard of those things," Danny said. "Are they demons?"

"No, they're a very rare sort of monster that kills people and takes their place. By eating the brain, they gain all the person's knowledge and they can shapeshift to look like them. That's likely what Richard is as well."

"King Miles didn't strike me as evil when we met."

"Despite the name, braineaters aren't evil. They're lazy. They take the place of the most powerful person they can, then live a life of ease and indulgence. I can't imagine what sort of deal they made with the cult of Ardent Lilly, but you can be sure it won't be good for us." Lyra tossed the head aside and set out for the door.

As Danny followed she asked, "How did you get the artifact? I didn't hear a fight."

"There wasn't one." Danny laid out what happened. "I'm not sure how he did it, but the priest vanished in a second."

"Probably some short-range teleportation spell. Why did you let him go?" Lyra sounded incredulous. "You don't have to honor a promise to a demon worshipper."

"You think I did him a favor? What do you imagine his superiors are going to do when they find out what he gave us? Killing him quickly would've been a kindness."

"That's harsher than I was expecting from you."

Danny shrugged and picked up the pace. "I'm not the hero anymore."

CHAPTER 20

Eve had never thought about how much food there was in a city. When she went to the market, there was always a good selection and that brought an end to her consideration. Over the past couple of weeks, her perspective had changed a great deal. The markets were all empty. The taverns were closed and people were keeping their pets inside and locked down. She hadn't seen a stray dog in a week.

Now, every morning, hungry people came to the temple district for bread. Eve and her fellow priests created it by channeling the archangels' power of creation. It was a very limited thing, and exhausting to use, but somehow, all of them working together had kept the populace from starving to death.

At least they had so far.

Eve slumped to the ground and leaned against the cool stone of Branik's temple. Since Thomas, the high priest of Branik, was in charge of their efforts, everyone agreed his temple was the best place to hand out food. The many large, armored men also kept the surly crowd polite and under control.

A gentle hand on her shoulder brought her instantly alert. She found Thomas's kind if exhausted face right above her. "You should go back to the cathedral. It looks like you could use a nap. We can't have you passing out on us tonight during the evening giveaway."

"I was just resting my eyes."

Thomas's eyes crinkled when he smiled. "Of course you were. Would you like one of my men to escort you?"

Eve forced herself to stand. "I'll be okay. It's a short walk. If I should sleep in, send someone to get me when it's time. I'll do my part."

"No one doubts that. I'd say you conjured more loaves than any three of us. You might be best known for summoning the hero, but the people of Villipan City will remember you forever for feeding them in this crisis."

Her cheeks warmed. "I didn't do any more than anyone else. We're all trying our best."

"So we are." Thomas made the sign of the inverted sword across his chest. "Branik watch over you."

Eve made the halo over her head. "Adonael watch over you."

She set off for the cathedral, her steps reasonably steady. The overwhelming exhaustion that came with channeling Adonael's power of creation always struck her as odd. She could do a lot more with her other spells before suffering any backlash, but that one thing knocked her out in a hurry. Likely it was one of those things that would always remain a mystery.

No one troubled her during her walk and she let out a sigh of relief when she stood once more in front of the Crystal Cathedral. She pushed the door open and strode through. The chapel was empty. No surprise there since Sister Rose was busy helping out at the Goddess's temple. Though older than Eve, she couldn't wield the power of creation. Not all priests could and that was yet another thing Eve didn't understand.

Right now, the main thing she understood was that she needed to reach her bed before she fell down. Slipping through the door to the back passages, she nearly walked face first into King Forte's chest.

"Beg your pardon, Majesty," she said.

"Not at all, Eve. I thought I heard something and sure enough it was you. How did it go today?"

"Well enough. Everyone who showed up for bread got a loaf and no fights broke out. All things considered, that's the best I can hope for. Where are Prince Florian and the others?"

"I believe they went out to speak with some noble acquaintances of theirs."

"You didn't wish to join them?" Eve asked.

He smiled, a gentle expression that warmed his haggard face. "I thought it best for at least one adult to remain behind with the little ones. Such sweet children. Do you know that I've never spent much time among elf-bloods? I'm not even sure if any live in Forte."

"I know their village is somewhere in Villipan, but not exactly where. Lady Shael is very circumspect when it comes to talking about her people."

"I thought you two were friends."

Eve shook her head. "I'm not sure she has any human friends. It must be hard to get close to someone when you know they'll die in a few decades while you continue on, unchanging, for eternity. It's sad and makes me glad I'm not immortal."

"I'd never thought about that." King Miles got a faraway look in his eyes before giving a little shake of his head. "You make a good point. Well, you look all in. I'll get out of your way so you can rest."

"Thank you, Your Majesty. Good day." Eve hurried on, the siren song of her bed calling.

As she went she couldn't help thinking that, for a king, Miles seemed like a decent fellow. Far less intimidating than King Richard. As soon as she thought it she felt bad. Eve resolved to offer a prayer for her soul before she fell asleep. You shouldn't speak ill of the dead.

Hopefully she'd be recovered enough by evening to keep any more people from joining him.

○

Nahia sat in a tower room she'd found one day while exploring Villipan Castle. It had an arrow slit that provided an excellent view of the court-yard and city beyond. Everything was peaceful at the moment. The shadow demons she'd dispatched to keep an eye on the populace informed her the temples were using Heavenly magic to create food for the masses. That was perfect for her as it kept many potential sacrifices alive for future slaughter and kept the priests too weak and worn out to try attacking her.

Of greater concern was the message she held in her lap. It had been delivered by a bone messenger a couple of hours ago. The hero and his elf-blood teacher had driven Durok out of Forte City. They had gone all that way to collect some magical artifact. His report didn't mention what the item did, only that it looked like a hoop made of metal perhaps a foot in diameter. He'd traded it for his life and the lives of his succubus familiars.

Whether that ended up being a good trade or not depended on what the hoop did. Nahia wasn't shocked Durok had given up without a fight. The man was a reasonably talented hellpriest, but he wouldn't last a minute against someone capable of defeating the demon king. Galling as it was to admit, neither would she.

The message ended with him letting her know he'd relocated to the processing center to help with transformations.

Nahia sighed. She should've expected the hero to go somewhere else to kill her servants given his inability to force his way through the barrier. In truth, the demon king's plan allowed for the possibility that everything other than Villipan City fell to the enemy. As long as she could reach the Crystal Cathedral, nothing else mattered.

A small figure appeared on the road approaching the castle. Nahia sharpened her vision. Occasionally one of the residents would come to the gate in the hope of getting food from the guards. They never did since she controlled the guards and they had orders not to share their food. Starving the population didn't work very well if your servants also handed out meals.

It was a ragged-looking woman rather than a kid as she first thought. A little smile played about Nahia's lips as the woman walked up to the guards. Her desperation turned to futile anger as she was turned aside. It was a beautiful sight.

She went back to her chair and settled in. The waiting was tedious, but she knew she had a long while to go before the demon king returned. It was fortunate she had little scenes like that to amuse her. Once everyone in the city was dead, it would no doubt get even more dull.

○

ve came awake to someone pounding on her door. She didn't know how long she'd been asleep beyond not long enough. A light appeared at her mental command. Her room had no window so she hadn't a clue what time it was.

More pounding interrupted her confused thoughts.

No one would be that insistent if it was just time for the evening bread line. She rolled out of bed and tried to rub the sleep from her eyes. Smacking both her cheeks didn't help either.

She walked over and yanked the door open just as Sister Rose was about to pound on it again. "What, in Adonael's name, is the problem?"

"The people are forming a mob with the intention of storming the castle. A woman from the slums approached the gate this morning and swore she could smell roasting meat. The guards refused to give her any. Rumors have been spreading and now the people are determined to get their share. Prince Florian tried to talk to them and barely escaped with his skin intact. If you can't turn them aside, no one can."

It took Eve a moment to process what she'd been told. "There are demons in the castle. If the people attack, they'll be slaughtered. Give me a second to change."

Eve closed the door and quickly swapped out her wrinkled work robe for the white-and-gold one she wore on Holy Day. She needed to look like a proper high priestess if she was going to have any chance of succeeding. Desperate, angry people didn't like listening to reason. They might not believe her, but, having seen what demons were capable of, Eve had to try and turn them aside.

With a final adjustment to her collar, she opened the door back up. "Where are they?"

"West's Tavern on Bell Street," Sister Rose said. "It's a straight shot from there to the castle. You have to hurry. According to the prince, they had about worked themselves up enough to attack."

"Right, I know where Bell Street is. Wish me luck."

"Adonael go with you."

Eve nodded. She dearly wished that were possible.

She left the cathedral behind and hurried deeper into the city. Fear had burned away the last of her fatigue. Once things calmed down she felt certain her exhaustion would return even stronger. But for now she welcomed the burst of energy.

Three blocks from the cathedral she heard angry voices. Angling toward them, she found a mob of several hundred people headed right up the main street. They were armed with kitchen utensils, clubs, and in one case a broom. It was a pitiful sight despite their numbers. In her mind's eye, Eve could see them all slaughtered, their bodies spread out on the ground in front of her. That couldn't be allowed to become reality.

Eve stood in their path and raised her arms to the side. She knew she didn't make the most impressive barricade, but they did stop a few feet from her. "Don't do this. The only thing waiting for you at the castle is death."

"They have meat!" someone shouted.

"The guards can't stop all of us," another said.

"There are demons in the castle and you're armed with cutlery." Eve shook her head. "Real soldiers would stand no chance against them. You will be slaughtered to the last person and accomplish nothing. I beg you, don't do this.

Come to the temple of Branik tonight. There will be bread for everyone."

"We're sick of bread!" a third person shouted. Others roared their approval.

An older man stepped out of the crowd and moved toward Eve. He carried a cleaver in his right hand. She swallowed hard but didn't back down.

"Stand aside, Priestess," he said, his voice gentle but firm. "We'll not be turned aside. Better to die fighting than to starve."

"As long as you're alive there's hope we'll find a way to free the city. Once you're dead, that's it. Even I can't help you."

"Your concern is much appreciated, lass. But we mean to do this. You'd best go on back to the cathedral. No sense in watching what's to come."

Eve looked into his eyes and saw both determination and acceptance. Nothing she could say would change his mind. These people knew they were likely going to their deaths and they'd accepted it on the faint hope that they might steal victory from the hands of death.

She made the sign of the halo in the group's direction. She hadn't recovered enough to do anything else for such a large group. "Adonael protect you."

And with that, Eve stepped out of the way. The older man offered her a faint smile then led the group on toward the castle. She waited until they'd gotten a decent lead then followed. Whatever happened, Eve felt it was her duty to bear witness. She would do her best to remember them.

All too soon, the walls were in sight. Instead of the usual guards on duty, four blackguards stood in front of the gate. Their black armor seemed to absorb the light. They held heavy, saw-toothed black iron swords at the ready.

With an inarticulate roar, the mob surged forward. What came next would haunt Eve's nightmares for the rest of her life. Screams of the dying filled the air. Every swing of the blackguards' swords cut two or three people in half. For their part, the mob's weapons couldn't so much as scratch the black armor.

It was a useless, pointless gesture. In five minutes the battle, if you could call it that, was over. Eve slipped silently away, tears streaming down her cheeks. She couldn't save them. She couldn't save anyone.

Eve sent a prayer heavenward. "Please, Adonael, let Daniel and Lady Shael return soon. Your useless servant is trying her best, but I need their help. Please."

CHAPTER 21

Danny had lost track of how many times he'd come back to Villipan City, but now he once more found himself approaching the western gate. The black dome covering everything looked the same. As before, they found no people or wagons in the area. He and Lyra had passed through a few villages on their way here and word had spread about the dome. People thought the city was cursed and wanted no part of it. That wasn't such a bad thing given the current circumstances, but hopefully they could convince everyone the curse had been lifted once the dome was gone.

"Do you know how to use that thing yet?" he asked.

Lyra had been studying the hoop every time they stopped for a rest. She said little to Danny, but from her furrowed brow and scowl, he wasn't optimistic about her progress.

"I have a basic understanding of how it works. As far as I can tell, you place it against the barrier you want to open and it does whatever it does." She sounded about as confident as high schooler giving his first book report in front of the class having not bothered to read the book.

"Maybe we should let Eve know we're back and have a chat with her wizard friend. If he knew the guy who made this thing, he might have some insight to offer."

"I prefer not to delay any further." Lyra ground her teeth and Danny knew how she felt.

"I get that, really. But what if we mess up and ruin the artifact? I have serious doubts there's another one lying around for us to find. A few more hours isn't going to make much difference. Better to do it once and do it right as the EOD guys back home used to say."

They reached the gate and Lyra turned to look at him. "EOD?"

"Explosive Ordnance Disposal. They disarmed bombs. Every one of them volunteered for the unit. Crazy, but brave. The point is, we don't want to rush and screw this up."

"Fine, we'll send another message stone to the cathedral. If she hasn't—"

"Excuse me!" A man in leather armor with a sword strapped to his back came running toward them. "Are you High Priestess Carre's friends? I was on the lookout for your return."

Danny nodded. "That's right. If you could let her know we're here and ask her to bring her wizard associate that would be very helpful."

"I'll see to it." He ran off into the city.

"I'm impressed she convinced the adventurers to work with her," Lyra said.

"Why?" Danny asked. "I've never met anyone that doesn't like Eve. Anyway, she probably posted a job asking for look-outs. I doubt it would cost very much."

Lyra shook her head. "I've never had much use for adventurers. They're all too busy looking for the next coin to see the bigger picture."

Danny smiled. So many replies came to mind he wasn't sure which one to go with.

"What are you smiling at?" she asked.

"I was just thinking how painful focusing on the bigger picture could be." Lyra had the good grace to wince. "Relax, I'm less pissed about what you did than I was at first. It helps that the person who ordered the job is dead, his brain having been devoured by some weird monster. A fitting end as far as I'm concerned. I hope it was as painful as it sounds. The only thing I regret is not having a chance to beat him half to death. But life is full of disappointment."

"You have no idea how right you are."

On that bitter note, he decided to change the subject. "Assuming this works, what's the plan once we're inside?"

"We're going straight to the cathedral. No way am I going to let that monster stay close to my granddaughters for a moment longer than necessary."

Danny figured she'd say that. "I'll head for the castle and try to take care of the priestess quickly."

"Do you want the hero's sword and armor?"

"No, the ethersword should be plenty. There can't be too many demons left. When I'm done, I'll meet you at the cathedral."

She nodded then said, "Here comes Eve."

Sure enough Eve, the grimy wizard, and a handful of adventurers were hurrying down the street. Danny felt certain Eve had introduced the wizard, but for the life of him he couldn't remember the man's name. Not surprising since they only met once and the situation was tense.

When they got closer Danny's jaw dropped. Eve looked

like she'd been through a war. Her face was pale and waxy, her eyes dark and bloodshot. Her robe wasn't in as bad a shape as the wizard's, but it was wrinkled and he could see bread crumbs here and there. It hadn't been that long since they parted company. What in the world had been happening?

"I'm so glad you're back," Eve said. "Did you find the artifact?"

Lyra pulled the hoop out of her storage. "We did. I wanted to consult with the guild master before we tried to activate it. There were no instructions on how to use the device when we found it."

"I'm glad you waited," the guild master said. "I spoke with my colleague extensively about the project. Please don't tell anyone. It was supposed to be a secret military project for the Forte government."

"Everyone likely to care is dead," Lyra said with typical brutal honesty. "How do we use it?"

"Right, okay," the guild master said. "First, place the hoop against the barrier. Don't let your skin touch it! Use telekinesis. As soon as it activates, end your spell. If everything goes as it's supposed to, the device should absorb the energy within the opening."

"Two questions," Lyra said. "What happens if it doesn't go smoothly and, assuming it does, how do we make the opening big enough for us to use?"

"I'll answer the second one first," he said. "As with all magic, you visualize the hoop getting bigger. It won't happen quickly and you'll be able to sense when it's reached maximum size. Don't try to push further as it might shatter. Bennett almost killed himself twice when some of his earlier efforts exploded."

Danny moved a couple steps further away. His original

body had been blown up once, he didn't need it to happen twice. Lyra shot him a dirty look before returning her focus to the project at hand.

"How will I know all this?" Lyra asked.

"As the one putting the artifact in place, you'll form a magical connection to it. Until it's deactivated or destroyed, you'll be the only one capable of manipulating it."

Lyra nodded. "Okay. And if I run into a problem?"

"This is the tricky bit. And it's why I'm glad you waited until I arrived to activate the artifact. If the energy flow isn't smooth, then the two of us, working from each side, have to iron it out."

"Elaborate," Lyra said.

"Basically…" The guild master started in on a long, detailed explanation.

While he was talking, Eve caught Danny's eye and nodded off to one side. When they reached the edge of the gate she said, "Did you understand all that?"

Danny snorted a laugh. "Hardly. I'm here to chew bubble gum and kill demons and I'm all out of bubble gum."

Eve stared at him. "What's bubble gum?"

"Forget it, that was a joke from my world. How are you holding up? No offense, but you look like hell."

"It's been rough. We've kept the populace from starving by the narrowest of margins, but it's left every priest capable of wielding the power of creation on the verge of collapse. If you'd been a week or maybe even a couple of days later, I shudder to think what might've happened."

"We're not out of the woods yet, but hopefully, even if we fail to bring down the barrier, this widget will let supplies enter the city. Not an ideal solution, but better than nothing."

Eve nodded. "Far better."

A loud crack drew their attention back to Lyra. She'd placed the artifact in position and now black sparks were shooting out of it. Though far from a master magician, Danny was pretty confident that black sparks shooting out of anything was a bad sign.

The adventurers appeared to agree as they were scrambling to put as much distance between themselves and the magical goings-on as possible.

"I don't know if you're up to a barrier," Danny said. "But if you can manage one, it might be a good idea. A few prayers wouldn't hurt either."

Eve already had her hands clasped in front of her.

Following his own advice, Danny conjured an invisible barrier. Hopefully Lyra knew her stuff. If they blew up the artifact, Danny didn't have a plan B.

◌

L yra couldn't say she blamed Daniel for moving a bit further away when she started activating the artifact. Though she'd been studying magic for most of her very long life, some of the wizard's explanations were too advanced even for her. Fortunately she did understand the basic theory, which should be enough to get her through. Or so she told herself. Might as well be optimistic since she had to do this either way.

Taking a deep breath, she guided the hoop into position using an ethereal tentacle. As soon as the dark metal touched the darker barrier, it adhered, and black sparks started shooting out of it. The energy flow was so ragged it would make a saw blade look smooth in comparison. It dispersed through the hoop in equally irregular waves.

Lyra focused on the hoop. As each wave hit, she smoothed it as best she could, guiding the energy to where it belonged. It took every drop of focus she could muster, but somehow she stabilized the pattern. Gradually the waves smoothed as well and soon the energy was flowing in a regular stream.

She dared look away from the ether long enough to see the guild master, brow furrowed in concentration, adjusting the corrupt energy as it reached the hoop. So that was the answer. She didn't know how strong he was in terms of raw power, but his skill at ethereal manipulation was beyond reproach.

When a hole big enough for a knitting needle to pass through opened up in the center of the hoop, she allowed herself a moment to breathe easy. Despite her misgivings it was working.

That momentary lapse in concentration nearly cost her. A wave of corruption came rushing through the barrier like a tidal wave of darkness. It broke on a wall of ether erected by the guild master, but massive amounts still reached the hoop. Lyra dispersed it as quickly and carefully as she could.

The metal vibrated and for a moment she feared it was going to shatter.

At her mental command, bands of ether formed, reinforcing the hoop's structural integrity. Corruption ate away at them, forcing her to constantly repair the damage. It felt like an endless struggle that probably only lasted half a minute.

And then the wave was gone and the opening in the hoop was big enough for her to stick her head through. Just a little bit more and the hoop was open.

"Well done." The guild master's voice startled her so much that she jumped. "I feared that when the creator's counterattack came, it would overwhelm us. In the end it sped the process. I recommend you take a break before trying to expand the opening."

"We don't have time," Lyra said.

"Take the time. Nothing's going to change in the next few hours. Rest, recover your strength. You have to be near backlash by now. Think how long it will take you to recover if you pass out halfway through the process. Or worse, lose your concentration and destroy the hoop."

Lyra wanted to snarl a curse at him, but she knew he was right. Taking a deep breath and letting it out slowly, she stepped back from the barrier. "Two hours and not a minute more."

The guild master bowed to her. "A wise decision."

"What was your name again?" Lyra asked.

"Guy Soyer. An absolute honor to work with you, Lady Shael."

"Likewise." Her legs wobbled and she dropped to the dirt.

Daniel ambled over and crouched beside her. "Can't say I understand much of what you did, but it looks like it took it out of you. How are you feeling?"

"Like I'd rather run to Forte City and back again than touch any more corrupted ether. But what I'd prefer is irrelevant. I'm going to open a path then I'm going to the cathedral to deal with those monsters before they can hurt my girls."

"I'll join you as quick as I can."

Lyra nodded. Much as she would've preferred they stick together, the sooner the priestess was dead, the sooner the barrier would fall.

Daniel opened his pocket dimension, using his body to shield it from view, and pulled out a water skin. "Here. Can't have you getting dehydrated."

"Thank you." She took a long pull and her eyes widened. It was ice cold.

When she looked at him she found Daniel grinning. "You're not the only one who knows a magical trick or two. Plus, I prefer my water cold. Wish I'd known how to do that back in my old world. Drinking piss-warm water in the middle of the desert isn't very refreshing. Though it does beat the alternative."

She took another long drink before passing the skin back. Lyra felt refreshed if not as energetic as she would've liked. "Once the city's secure, I'm taking a couple days to rest."

"That's a plan I can get behind. Though I am looking forward to returning to Rosenbar, collecting my pay, and seeing about that grand caravan Trevor mentioned."

"You're still determined to leave on your fool's errand?"

He shrugged. "Nothing's changed. I said I'd see this through and I will, but once we settle with the priestess, I'm moving on. No more innocents from my world will die if I can prevent it."

Hearing the steel in his voice convinced her to drop the subject. Lyra doubted she had any hope of changing his mind in any case.

A bit of quiet rest did wonders to restore her strength and at last she stood and said, "I'm ready."

Guy was waiting for her beside the artifact. "I fear I can't help you with this last part. But I will keep watch for any more counterattacks. Don't forget, as soon as you feel the hoop starting to fracture, stop. You've reached the maximum diameter."

That was hardly something she was likely to forget, but she appreciated the warning all the same.

Lyra reached out and touched the hoop through the ether. The artifact wasn't self-aware, but it did sort of resonate with her thoughts. She pictured it getting bigger, slowly expanding to make the opening big enough to step through. Inch by inch it grew and as it did, the metal got thinner. That made sense. It would've required earth magic or creation magic to increase the hoop's mass and neither of them was woven into the metal.

When the hoop grew as thin as a barrel strap she stopped. It was practically quivering with the strain. They'd have to duck, but she and Daniel could enter now.

Lyra took a step. Finally on the other side of the barrier, she wobbled. A strong hand on her elbow steadied her. "You sure you're up to this?" Daniel asked.

"I'll manage." Lyra hated the weakness in her voice.

Eve hurried over to them. "I can help. Hold on."

She pressed her palms to Lyra's cheeks. Warmth and strength flowed into her. Lyra straightened and pulled away from Daniel. "I'm okay now. Thank you, Eve."

Eve took her hands away, her expression gloomy. "You're welcome, but you need to know there'll be a price to pay later. When the spell wears off, you're going to be even weaker than you are now."

"This will be settled in a couple hours at most. Let's get to the cathedral. I need to have a word with King Miles."

○

A sudden lance of agony through Nahia's midriff made her double over. She generally enjoyed a bit of pain, though she much preferred to dish it out than to receive it, but this was torment unlike anything she'd ever experienced. She soon recovered.

She sent her magical focus inward and traced the source of the pain back to the barrier. Someone, somehow, had opened a hole in it. That shouldn't be possible given how much power ten hell portals could provide. But impossible or not, it *was* happening. And she needed to nip it in the bud right now. If the lockdown was broken, all her efforts would be for nothing.

A mental command sent a stream of concentrated corruption surging toward whatever dared interfere with her barrier. It connected, but the impact was diffused and the damage continued to grow. As the opening got bigger, the pain grew as well. It was like her essence was being ripped apart along with the barrier. Which wasn't wrong considering how tightly she was bound to it.

Her attack continued to no avail until exhaustion forced her to stop. Nahia panted for breath and hugged herself. It didn't help since the pain was more psychic than physical. But there was something that would.

She summoned the nearest servant. They were constantly scurrying around, carrying out their useless tasks as if nothing was wrong. She sometimes found it amusing. Twisting people's minds was something Nahia enjoyed.

A couple minutes later a dumpy woman in a servant's smock pushed the door open. "Yes, Mistress?"

"Come here."

As soon as she was within reach, Nahia touched her forehead and sent a thread of ether into her. The servant went rigid as Nahia's pain flowed into her. When it was done, Nahia was back to normal and the servant lay twitching on the floor, her mind overcome.

Nahia shook her head. Had she been so pathetic once? It embarrassed her to admit she had. Putting aside the unpleasant memories of her time before coming to serve Ardent Lilly, Nahia dove back into the barrier. What she found horrified her. The gap was growing wider by the second. Some sort of metal hoop was absorbing the corruption and using it to grow the opening.

Wait, didn't Durok say the hero came to Forte in order to claim a metal hoop? This must be the same artifact. And the fool had just handed it over. She ground her teeth in annoyance. Who was she kidding? Durok had no more hope of stopping the hero than he did the sunrise. He did what he had to in order to survive.

That wouldn't prevent Nahia from punishing him when next they met.

Refocusing, she honed in on the person controlling the hoop's magic. She recognized the elf-blood bitch at once. However valuable her blood might have been, Nahia wished she'd just killed her when she had the chance.

There were other presences nearby, but since they weren't connected to the barrier, she couldn't get any details. Still, she felt certain that if the elf-blood was here, the hero had to be as well. And given the speed at which the gap was growing, it wouldn't be long before the duo paid her a visit.

Nahia's troops were more than enough to deal with rabble, but they wouldn't trouble the hero in the least. Much like Durok, if she wanted to survive, it was time to relocate.

Ignoring the still-twitching servant, Nahia made her way to the first floor. The braineater had served its purpose and she couldn't bring the horrid creature with her in any case. The blackguards and thralls would have to remain behind as well. Only the succubus could fly so it would be just the two of them.

The demon appeared beside her as she strode through the entry hall. It asked no questions, simply following along. Extremely intelligent and absolutely loyal, the demon knew better than to speak given Nahia's wretched mood.

As soon as they reached the courtyard, Nahia opened a

gap in the top of the barrier and conjured ebony wings from her back. She leapt and beat them hard. Soon she and the demon were soaring away from Villipan City.

But it was only a temporary setback. As long as she lived, the barrier would remain. And when the time came, she swore she'd return with an army so huge even the hero wouldn't be able to stop her from reclaiming it.

CHAPTER 22

Danny walked along beside Eve and Lyra toward the turnoff to the castle. He'd assumed Lyra would be off at a dead sprint, but given the shape she was in, power walking seemed about the best she could manage. Hopefully those braineater things weren't too tough. It didn't sound like they were. Danny didn't know what he might run into at the castle, but even at eighty percent of his full strength, he figured he'd be okay. The only thing that shook his confidence was the priestess's ability to hide. He'd missed her once and didn't want to do so again.

"You're an adventurer too, right?" Danny turned his attention to a man only a fraction smaller than the crimson ogres he'd killed. He towered a foot over Danny, but didn't give off an intimidating vibe. Though that would no doubt change should the situation require it.

"That's right. I'm Ronin, from the Rosenbar guild. Lady Shael hired me to work for her as a scout, though I've done a hell of a sight more fighting than I have scouting. It's a relief to see an end to the job."

"Leo. I imagine it's tough fighting beside a legend. The Golden Claws have been lucky to work with High Priestess Carre. I was a bit nervous when I first spoke to her, but she's been kind and pleasant whenever we're with her."

Danny nodded. "I've worked with her a bit on this job as well and can't fault your description. She seems like a sweetheart. I'm not sure if it's considered bad manners to ask this of a fellow adventurer, but if you could keep an eye on both of them until we meet up again, I'd be much obliged."

Leo clapped him on the shoulder, staggering Danny a step. "Count on the Golden Claws. Where are you going?"

"To scout the castle. Gotta figure out what we're up against." Danny kept the "and deal with it" to himself.

"That sounds sketchy as hell. Don't do anything crazy. I can send a couple of the boys with you if you think backup would be helpful."

"I appreciate the offer, but I'll be using a stealth field to stay invisible. No one will even know I'm there."

They reached the turnoff and Danny said, "This is where we part company. I'll catch up with you at the cathedral as soon as I'm finished."

"Be careful," Eve said.

Danny grinned at her. "I'm the very soul of caution."

He activated the stealth field and turned up the road, silent and invisible.

As soon as he left the others behind, Danny narrowed his focus to the matter at hand. While he was confident about what he was going to run into, that was by no means a guarantee. He'd been confident in Moreton as well.

Halfway to the castle gate he took the ethersword out of storage. This was not the place for half measures. Twenty yards from the gate, he froze. Scores of corpses littered the ground. They'd begun to rot and a few crows that must've been trapped inside the dome were busy picking at them. He had no idea what could've possessed regular citizens to attack the castle, but clearly it hadn't worked out for them.

Picking his way through the battlefield, Danny reached the open, unguarded gate. He'd expected to run into trouble here. Perhaps the priestess had massed all her guardians at the keep entrance. Danny was doubly grateful he'd thought to destroy the doors on their last visit. That would make getting inside much easier.

As soon as he entered the courtyard, Danny spotted ten thralls and four black-armored knights standing in front of the keep entrance. Not the most intimidating force compared to what he'd seen.

Ten yards away he let the stealth field fade and lit the ethersword. The white blade crackled to life.

As if that was a signal, all the demons charged.

Danny kicked his physical enhancement into third gear and got to work. The thralls were easy. Every slash cut one of them down. They were slow and stupid, exactly the sort of enemies he preferred to fight.

The blackguards put up a better fight. Their swords and armor could withstand a couple blows from the ethersword. But they were still too slow to hit Danny with a coun-terattack.

In less than a minute he'd put them all down and strode on toward the entrance. Nothing else attacked him and when he activated his magic he could sense a number of life forces. None of them felt corrupted like the priestess would've. Unfortunately, he also couldn't differentiate between the dominated humans and the braineater pretending to be the king.

With a little shrug he made his way to the royal suite. He doubted the monster would be dumb enough to hide somewhere so obvious, but it was a good place to start. He passed a few servants going about their business like everything was normal. All of them were psychically compromised. If he hadn't been able to see it in the ether, the fact that they ignored a man with a magical sword to focus on laundry would've been a dead giveaway.

Danny reached the royal suite without issue and kicked the door open. He found the false king lounging in an over-stuffed chair, a bottle of wine in his hand, and his feet up on the coffee table. Richard—it seemed easiest to think of the creature by the king's name for the moment—looked at him through bleary eyes.

"I wondered which of you was going to show up to kill me. I figured the elf-blood was more likely. It's an honor to be killed by the hero himself."

"You're drunk," Danny said.

"I certainly am. Dying sober has no appeal at all."

Danny wasn't sure what to make of this creature. "Where's the priestess?"

"Gone. Fled with her pet demon to hell knows where. I never should've taken this job. Demon worshippers are a disloyal bunch. They use you and abandon you without a thought. But the chance to become a king was too delicious to pass up. The fact that she would've killed me and my entire clan had we refused helped convince me as well."

"I'll bet." Danny saw no lie in any of the creature's words. He couldn't decide if this thing was evil or not. Killing and impersonating people seemed pretty evil, but if that was how they survived, he wasn't sure if he was in any position to judge. People killed each other for various reasons all the time.

"I do have one request. If at all possible, could you make it painless? One quick blow to end it?"

"I'm not going to kill you."

Richard's eyes got huge. "You're not?"

Danny shook his head. "No. And in exchange, you're going to tell us everything you know about the demon king's plans. You're damn lucky you didn't murder anyone I like. I might well have killed the king myself had he still been alive."

"Not a very heroic sentiment."

"I'm not the hero anymore. I'm Ronin, an adventurer. If anyone asks, that's what you tell them. Break that rule and I'll kill you in the slowest way I can think of."

"Hey, you're the boss. If that's how you want it, I'm glad to oblige." Richard sounded as happy as he had morose a few minutes go.

"Come on, we're going to the cathedral. Maybe I can convince Lyra to spare your relatives." Though all things considered, Danny wasn't optimistic.

⟳

With the energy from Eve's spell flooding through her, Lyra felt more energetic than she had since entering Forte City. She'd been warned it would exact a price, but Lyra was willing to pay it. She had to make sure the girls were okay. And the quickest way was to eliminate the braineaters.

"Are you sure about this?" Eve asked. "King Forte has been a model guest. Nothing he's done suggests that he's anything other than what he claims."

"You say that because you haven't seen his corpse and the hole in its skull. I assure you King Miles is dead and very shortly the thing impersonating him will be as well."

"Is it okay for Ronin to go to the castle by himself?" Leo asked. "Some nasty things live up there."

It took Lyra a moment to remember he was talking about Daniel. The magic that gave her strength also seemed to be addling her wits. It was either that or lack of sleep.

"Ronin is very talented," she said. "That's the reason I hired him. Rest assured, he'll be fine. If the threat is too great, he'll retreat and come get me."

She couldn't imagine what Daniel might encounter that would make him retreat, but best to keep that thought to herself.

Leo shot another look at the castle, his huge brow furrowed.

"I'm surprised you're so worried," Lyra said. "You two just met."

"Professional courtesy," Leo said. "We're both adventurers. That creates a certain brotherhood. No one else can fully appreciate what you deal with on a regular basis. You might think that since people in our profession die so often we'd get numb to it, but the truth is, every death reminds you your own could be right around the corner."

Lyra never expected such a philosophical comment from an adventurer. She considered them all drunken mercenaries. Apparently she'd underestimated them, or some of them at any rate. The group's arrival at the cathedral spared her from further conversation.

The doors opened as they approached and Lyra charged ahead. In the chapel, to her absolute horror, the girls were sitting in a pew on either side of the fake king. She couldn't make out what he was saying, but they both looked happy.

The girls looked her way and big smiles crossed their faces. "Grandma!" they said in unison.

The fraud made no move to stop them as they ran over and hugged her. Lyra patted their heads but never took her eyes off the braineater. It looked back at her with sad eyes.

"Where've you been?" Tara asked.

"Ronin and I had to take a trip to Forte so we could make an opening in the barrier. Are you two okay?"

"We're fine, Grandma," Nora said. "Eve takes good care of us and Mr. Miles tells the best stories."

"Is that right? I'm glad you two had fun."

The fake king stood. "They're sweet kids. It's been a joy interacting with them. How did you find things in Forte?"

"Bad. Really bad." Lyra took her hand off Tara's head and placed it on the hilt of her sword. "We found some mangled remains."

"How unfortunate."

"Indeed, most unfortunate. Girls, why don't you go play with Eve?"

Tara and Nora both looked up at her, clearly confused.

"What's going on?" Nora asked.

Lyra wasn't sure how to explain it to them so she said, "Miles isn't who you think he is. He's dangerous and it's my job to deal with dangerous things."

They pulled away from her and hurried to stand in front of the braineater, arms raised to the side to block her. "Mr. Miles is our friend," Tara said.

"You can't hurt him," Nora added.

"Girls, get out of the way." Lyra used her best I'm-not-joking parent voice. "He may not look it now, but that thing is dangerous."

"He's nice," Tara said. "Talk to him, Grandma. You'll see."

Lyra found it equal parts adorable and exasperating to have her granddaughters standing up for a monster. She was proud of them for doing what they thought was right, but that didn't change what had to happen.

The braineater patted Tara and Nora on the head, a gentle smile on his face. "It's okay, little ones. The time I've spent playing with you has been one of the few joys of my life. Best run along now. The grownups have important things to talk about."

"You can't fight Grandma," Nora said.

The braineater shook its head, smile never wavering. "I have no intention of fighting her. Run along now."

The girls hesitated, looking from her to the monster and back. It stabbed Lyra's heart to think they were more worried about that thing than her. No, she wasn't being fair. They were young and didn't appreciate the danger. They'd understand when they got older.

At last Tara said, "Don't hurt him, Grandma. Mr. Miles really is nice."

The girls took a step toward the back of the chapel.

"Wait," Lyra said. "Where's the rest of the royal family?"

"I believe Prince Florian and his sisters are out visiting a noble acquaintance," Eve said.

"My clanmates are in our room," the braineater said. "I can call them if you wish."

"Do so. Eve, can you take the girls somewhere safe?"

"I'd like to hear what's discussed," Eve said.

"I won't get started until you return."

Eve nodded and held out her hands. She led the girls into the back of the cathedral.

When the door closed behind them, the braineater looked right at her. "It's good that you waited until they were gone. This isn't the sort of thing children should see."

"You seem calm given the circumstances," Lyra said. "Do you not plan to fight back?"

"My kind are poor at combat. If I ambushed you, maybe I'd have a chance, but a straight-up fight?" He shook his head. "I wouldn't last five seconds."

Lyra wasn't sure what to think, but she didn't trust this

thing as far as she could throw a castle. It had to be up to something.

Two people dressed in fine gray robes emerged from the door Eve had just led the girls through. They looked like an older woman, and a boy about Daniel's age. There really was nothing to distinguish them from a normal person. Lyra found that more terrifying than the demons.

Eve returned a couple minutes later and moved to stand beside Lyra. "They're in my room and I warded the door."

"Thank you." Turning her attention to the braineaters, Lyra said, "I want to hear everything. When you're finished, I'll decide whether or not to kill you."

"As you wish," Miles said. "Several years ago, the demon king approached my clan. She offered us positions of power and ease in exchange for helping her take control of Villipan City. I personally dislike working with demon worshippers, but our clan leader was eager to take her up on the offer. Since we are all obedient to his orders, the deal was done."

"Your clan leader, he's the one impersonating Richard?" Lyra asked.

Miles nodded. "He insisted on the position, believing it would provide the best food and the most comfort. I'm pleased we ended up here. Our clan leader is not fond of children."

"And what, exactly, was your mission?" Lyra asked.

"We were to remain here until the demon king returned. When she made her move against the cathedral, we were to strike down all the priests of Adonael who might try and oppose her. We had no orders regarding your granddaughters or the surviving Villipan royals."

Eve let out a strangled sound. It wasn't every day you heard that the guests you'd been sheltering had orders to kill you at the appropriate time.

"And that's it?" Lyra asked. "That's all you know?"

"That's all we needed to know to complete our mission. Given our exposure to the enemy, it was deemed wise to keep as many details secret from us as possible."

A reasonable precaution, Lyra was forced to admit. It seemed she wasn't going to learn anything of value from this creature. She was also forced to admit that it didn't seem like a terrible person, leaving aside its orders to kill Eve. Lyra was enough of a soldier to acknowledge that good people sometimes did bad things. Either that or she was mentally trying to justify what she did to the heroes as just following orders.

As she stood there debating the best course of action, Eve turned toward the door. It opened a moment later and she smiled. "Da… I mean, Ronin is back and he's got company."

Lyra spun and watched as Daniel dragged a ragged-looking Richard into the cathedral. She hadn't expected him to return with a prisoner. "Why is he still alive?"

Daniel nodded toward Miles. "Why is he?"

Lyra winced. "We were discussing his orders. Plus, it seems the girls have taken a liking to him. As such I'm somewhat reluctant to run him through."

Daniel shrugged. "The priest and one of her pet demons fled. This one knows what she's up to. I figured it would be best for you to handle the questioning."

"If she's gone," Eve said. "Why is the barrier still up?"

"She's still connected to it," Guy said. "I don't know what the range will be, but given the power we're talking about, I'd wager she can go anywhere in the Five Kingdoms without issue."

The guild master had been so quiet Lyra had almost forgotten he was here. The Golden Claws were keeping their mouths shut as well. She appreciated that.

"I know where she's gone," Richard said.

Daniel gave him a shove and he ended up sprawled on the floor.

"No need to be so rough." The creature picked itself up and smoothed its stolen robes. "She's gone to their processing facility and the bitch wouldn't take me with her. After all my clan has done to help. Oh, greetings, brothers."

Miles and the other Forte frauds bowed to Richard before Miles said, "Clan chief. It's good that you're still alive."

"Spare me your lies. Nothing would make you happier than to see my desiccated body."

"Not at all. So few of us remain that even the death of someone stupid enough to trust the word of a demon worshipper diminishes the clan."

"It was too good of a deal to pass up! And do you think the demon king would've smiled and left us in peace had we refused? She'd have slaughtered us all!"

Miles shrugged. "We'll never know for sure. And now we're at the mercy of her enemies."

"At least, unlike the demon king, her enemies know the meaning of mercy," Richard countered.

"Enough!" Daniel shouted. "Tell us everything the psycho bitch has planned."

"If you mean the demon king," Richard said. "I fear I don't know much. As soon as she recruited us, she turned us over to Nahia—that's the priestess in charge of the Five Kingdoms' campaign. The one who abandoned me."

"Noted," Daniel said. "Now spill it."

Lyra didn't know if Daniel realized he'd taken over despite posing as a simple hired scout. She suspected he was acting on instinct. And that was fine with her. Pretending not to be the hero was a waste of time. Even if the whole kingdom learned the hero survived, they couldn't stop him from leaving if he wanted to.

"Fine," Richard said. "Humans are so impatient. Nahia's followers have built a huge processing facility to turn the people of Forte and eventually all of the Five Kingdoms into a demon army. Once the demon king takes down the cathedral and banishes Heaven from this world, they'll march outwards, claiming the entire world for Ardent Lilly. At least that was the plan. It was going pretty well, too. Her forces outside the city have already eliminated the army's scattered forces. Forte is pretty much depopulated. I'm not sure which kingdom they mean to move on next, but given what they already have at their disposal, none are likely to survive."

Lyra had expected the news to be grim, but this was worse than anything she'd imagined. As she considered the news, the room started to spin. She blinked, trying to stabilize her vision. Darkness nudged in from all sides and her legs got weak.

The next thing she knew she was staring up at Daniel's face. "What…"

"It's nap time for you. I'll keep an eye on our new friends, so get some sleep."

That struck her as an excellent idea. Lyra closed her eyes and was soon dead to the world.

CHAPTER 23

Holding a sound-asleep Lyra in his arms, Danny turned to the adventurers. "Would you guys mind keeping an eye on this lot? I need to put Lady Shael to bed."

"Is she okay?" Leo asked.

"She's exhausted," Eve said. "I used my magic to keep her going, but the spell has run its course. She will likely sleep for a full day, possibly more."

"Some people have all the luck," Danny muttered. "I'll take her back to wherever you left the girls. I'm sure they're wondering what's going on."

"Don't worry," Leo said. "We won't let them out of our sight."

"Thanks." Danny turned a hard glare on the braineaters. "Don't make me regret letting you live."

Richard raised his hands in a placating gesture. "We'll be on our best behavior, rest assured."

That was what worried him, but Lyra was getting heavy

so Danny nodded and made his way to the door. Eve hurried to follow along beside him.

As she led him down a stone hall Danny asked, "You okay?"

"Of course, why?"

"The way the blood drained from your face when Miles said his job was to kill you, I feared you might faint."

Eve's cheeks reddened. "I was shocked, though once I knew their real identities, perhaps I shouldn't have been. What are you going to do with them?"

"Keep an eye on them for now. Long term, no idea. When we leave, they won't be staying anywhere near you or the girls, that's for sure. This city must have some kind of a jail other than the castle dungeon. Maybe we could stick them in there. Given what they are, letting them go strikes me as an excellent way for some poor soul to end up murdered and his brain eaten. Killing them outright is an option, but not one I plan to carry out."

"Why?" Eve asked. "I mean, they are monsters at the end of the day. Exterminating monsters is something adventurers do, right?"

"You're not wrong, but killing some ogre that's running around the countryside burning villages and eating people seems different than killing something capable of reason. The braineaters are smart. Seems like there ought to be some way to make use of them. But as I said, it's not my decision and I'm fine with that."

They reached a door that glowed in the ether. Eve waved a hand in front of it then pushed it open. The girls came running out. They looked at the unconscious Lyra with wide, worried eyes.

"Is Grandma okay?" Tara asked.

"She's fine, kiddo." Danny strode into the bedroom and

looked from the nice, clean bedspread to Lyra's dusty traveling clothes. "Eve, do you have an old blanket or something you could put down? Neither of us has taken a bath in way too long and I don't want to make a mess of your bed."

"Don't worry about it," Eve said. "The younger priestesses clean them with magic as part of their training."

Danny wasn't about to argue. He laid Lyra down and let out a breath of relief. "Where are the other priestesses? I've only seen you and Sister Rose."

"The others don't live at the cathedral. They're scattered around the city so they can do good works like healing people in their neighborhoods or whatever. Some of them come in to help out once a week, and everyone is here on Holy Day. But otherwise they live their own lives."

"Pretty relaxed policy."

Eve smiled. "Unlike the temples of Branik and the Binder, Adonael's faith isn't militaristic. Our goal is to help as many people as we can. We're much more like the Goddess's faith in that regard, we just go about it in a different way."

One of the girls tugged on his pant leg and he looked down at Nora. "What's on your mind?"

"Is Mr. Miles okay?"

"Yeah, he's fine. You convinced Lyra to leave him alone." For the moment, Danny didn't add.

Both girls beamed at him.

"Can we go see him?" Tara asked.

"Actually, I was hoping you two would stay here and keep an eye on your grandmother for me. If she wakes up and needs anything, I'll be counting on you."

They both offered big nods. In Danny's experience, limited as it was, kids loved it when adults gave them a task they felt was important.

He patted both their heads. "I knew I could count on you two. Eve and I will be back in a bit to check on things."

They left the girls to watch over Lyra and closed the door. Eve restored the barrier protecting them and the pair turned back to the chapel.

"Lady Shael isn't the only one who needs to rest," Eve said. "You look exhausted."

Danny raised an eyebrow. "Pot calling the kettle black? Of the two of us, I'd say you're in more need of rest than me. I've only been fighting demons. You've got the pressure of feeding an entire city."

"I had a lot of help," Eve said.

"Me too."

They stared at each other for a second then started laughing. It felt good. Danny couldn't remember the last time he laughed with genuine amusement rather than bitterness.

When he got himself under control he wiped the tears away and said, "I'll rest once we deal with the braineaters."

They emerged from the back rooms to find Prince Florian and his sisters staring at the fake Richard, their mouths slightly open.

"Maybe you'd better handle this, Eve," Danny said under his breath.

"Majesty," Eve said.

Florian snapped his jaw shut and rounded on her. Danny tensed. Prince or not, if he tried to hurt Eve, Danny would stop him.

"Why is that demon here? I thought their kind couldn't enter the cathedral," Florian said.

"They're not demons, they're a sort of monster called a braineater. As to why they're here, the one posing as your father has worked closely with the priestess in charge of

Villipan City. We've been questioning him and in the process gained valuable information."

Florian had calmed a fraction as Eve spoke, though from his red face and clenched fists, his anger was still close to the surface. "And where is Lyra?"

"Sleeping. She's been going nonstop for days." Eve shook her head. "It's a wonder she didn't collapse before now. She should wake up in a day or so. We were planning to hold them in the guardhouse for now in case she has any more questions."

Florian looked like he wanted to punch something, but he kept himself under control. "Maybe you'd better tell me what happened."

Eve turned to Danny, who swallowed a sigh. "Majesty, my name is Ronin, we met briefly during our first visit to the city. Lady Shael has employed me as a scout."

"I remember. Tell me what you two have been doing."

Danny took a deep breath and launched into his story. He made sure to edit it to make Lyra sound like the one who did most of the fighting. Florian stayed quiet as he spoke, something that Danny much appreciated.

When he finished Danny said, "And that's how we got into the city. The opening seems stable, so supplies can be brought in. The people may want to leave and I couldn't blame them, but given what's happening in the countryside, I wouldn't recommend it."

"That," Florian said, "was a remarkable story. You have our gratitude for taking on such a dangerous assignment. What is Lady Shael's plan to deal with this, what did you call it, processing facility?"

"If she has a plan for it," Danny said. "She hasn't told me. It may be something she comes up with once she wakes up and speaks with the prisoners further. I fear, given our lack of resources, it will be a difficult task."

"I have no doubt." Florian ran his fingers through his hair. "Fine, I'll grant the monsters a reprieve until after Lyra speaks with them, but I want them out of the cathedral this instant. I can't stand the thought of sharing a roof with the horrid things."

Danny bowed. "As you wish, Majesty. Leo, can you show me the way to the nearest guardhouse?"

"Sure," the huge adventurer said. All the members of the Golden Claw had been silent, their gazes locked on the floor, since Florian arrived. "It's five blocks north of here. We'll help you lock them up."

"Thanks." Danny turned back to Florian. "With your permission, Majesty, we'll escort them to a secure space at once."

Florian waved them off. "The sooner the better."

Danny motioned the braineaters toward the door and they were all too happy to hurry along. Outside, the Golden Claws fell in around them with Leo in the front. Danny moved to walk along beside him.

They managed a full block before Leo asked, "Who are you really?"

"I'm a journeyman adventurer. I can show you my guild card if you don't believe me."

"I believe you have a card which says that, but no journeyman adventurer talks to a prince, a thousand-year-old elf-blood, and the high priestess of Adonael as easily as you do. Lady Shael scares the hell out of me and I could hardly squeeze a word out with Prince Florian present. Eve is easier. She seems like a regular person. Makes you want to protect her."

Danny shrugged. "I don't know what to tell you. I've

never been easily scared or impressed. They're all just people and only Lady Shael is truly dangerous. The prince might bark orders, but there's no one left to carry them out. What's he going to do, fight us himself?"

"That's what I mean," Leo said. "Your attitude toward a royal immediately marks you as something different from a common adventurer. Were you a noble who was forced to leave his home or something?"

"Sure, let's go with that if it makes you feel better." Danny had no intention of sharing his secret with someone he barely knew.

The walk to the guardhouse didn't take long. The single-story stone building was nothing to get excited about. Blocky and gray, Danny figured it was about a thousand square feet. The heavy wooden door was wide open so they went in. Danny sensed no life force; clearly the guards had called it quits. It seemed everyone that kept order in the city had found something else to do. It was a wonder there weren't riots or roving gangs of looters.

Maybe everyone was too weak from hunger. A useful side effect of starvation, not that he would recommend it as a broad policy.

To the left of the door was a desk and chair. Beyond that a wall with an iron door. A few feet away a large key hung from a nail driven into a support column. Danny gave a little shake of his head and grabbed the key. The iron door was unlocked and beyond it waited a double row of four cells.

Using the key, he unlocked the first on the right. With a jerk of his thumb Danny said, "In you get."

The braineaters shuffled into the cell and Danny slammed it shut. As he was locking it Richard said, "What gives you the right to call us monsters anyway? We're as intelligent as humans."

The lock clunked into place and he withdrew the key. "Intelligence has nothing to do with it. You murder people, eat their brains, then impersonate them. How is that anything but monstrous?"

"Humans murder people all the time," Richard countered. "Is it the brain eating specifically which offends you?"

"No, I consider humans who commit murder to be monsters as well. We generally either hang them or cut off their heads. Keep that in mind."

Without another word, Danny turned toward the exit. Back in the first room, he hung the key in its place.

"What now?" Leo asked.

"I'll arrange for someone to feed them. If you guys could rotate through the day to keep an eye on them, that would be a huge help. It shouldn't take more than two days for Lady Shael to fully recover. I can arrange a contract at the guild if you wish."

Leo shook his head. "We agreed to help Eve for free. We'll take care of this end."

"Thanks," Danny said. "I'm heading back to the cathedral. If you have any problems, send word. Otherwise, I'll be back when we're ready to talk to them again."

He shook hands with Leo and left the guardhouse. As soon as he was outside, Danny let out a jaw-cracking yawn. Lyra had the right idea; a few hours' sleep would be just the thing.

CHAPTER 24

Nahia flew west as fast as her Black Wings spell would carry her. Much as she hated abandoning the city, she knew there was no chance of her defeating the hero and the elf-blood with the forces at her disposal. Speaking of, she'd sensed the death of her thralls and blackguards. As expected, they hadn't lasted long. Now all that remained of her personal forces was the single succubus flying beside her. As the leader of all the demon king's forces in the Five Kingdoms, she could take whatever she wanted, but it felt pathetic to lose them all the same.

"What will we do now, Mistress?" the succubus asked.

"We will prepare for the hero's arrival. And when he arrives, we will make him suffer for interfering with the demon king's plan."

"How, when he's so strong? I doubt the thrall army will be enough."

"I suspect you're correct. That's why we're going to summon something more powerful than the hero. Even if it costs us all the sacrifices we've collected so far, the price will be worth it."

"Does such a demon exist?"

"Of course it does!" Nahia snapped at the demon, betraying her own doubts in the process. Despite trying to sound confident, she wasn't sure if they had enough sacrifices to summon a demon that powerful. In the end, all she could do was offer them all up and hope whatever demon Ardent Lilly sent would suffice.

They flew through the day and night. Nahia used her connection to the barrier to power her spell for far longer than she would've been able to on her own. Her maximum power level hadn't increased, but her stamina had.

Eventually she spotted the processing center, a huge but crude stone fortress her servants had built with magic. It was roughly situated at the intersection of Villipan, Forte, and Guilton for easy access to the maximum number of sacrifices.

She landed in the courtyard and let out a silent sigh of relief as the Black Wings spell ended. A quick look around made her feel better. Several thousand newly made thralls filled a quarter of the space. They stood around with blank looks on their faces waiting for orders. Pity they hadn't found some way to make the stupid things more useful.

Nahia shook her head and made her way to the keep, a two-story rectangle with a single door and no windows. The demon hurried ahead of her and pulled the door open. Nahia didn't even break stride as she entered.

The ground floor was a single giant room with a massive spell circle in the center. It could transform a dozen thralls at a time. It should also be big enough to allow some sort of huge demon to pass through. Despite her worries, Nahia was also excited to see one of her mistress's more powerful servants in the real world. It should be something.

"Mistress Nahia?" She looked up and found Durok standing on the walkway that circled the first floor. The handsome priest was an occasional playmate of hers, but right now she wasn't in the mood for pleasure. Pain, on the other hand, was definitely on the menu.

For him.

She strode over to the staircase leading to the walkway, her face set in a grim scowl. When she reached the top Durok had come to greet her.

"I didn't expect you to le—"

A blast of dark energy slammed into him and sent him flying across the walkway. Durok looked up at her, blood trickling down his lip. "What have I done to offend, Mistress?"

"Remember the trinket you gave up to save your miserable life? Do you know what it does?" He shook his head. "It opened a gap in my barrier. It allowed the hero and the elf-blood to enter. It forced me to flee!"

"I didn't know."

The truth she sensed in his words did nothing to soothe her anger. "I should kill you for your failure."

"When the hero arrives," Durok said, "you'll need all the help you can get. My death will gain you nothing."

He was right, damn the man. "Fine. I have more important things to spend my power on. How many sacrifices are in the dungeon?"

"The dungeon is nearly full. The raiding parties bring in more every few days. We can barely keep space open for the new arrivals."

"Perfect." Nahia told him her plan. "We'll need to alter the symbol to summon a single powerful demon rather than weak spirits. Once that's done, it's simply a matter of sacrificing all the prisoners in one shot."

"What about building up the army?" Durok asked.

"The army doesn't matter if the hero wipes out all the thralls. There are plenty of people in the Five Kingdoms. A few thousand more or less won't matter in the grand scheme of things."

Durok lowered his gaze in submission. "As you say, Mistress. Do you know which demon you will summon?"

"Not yet. I have to pray to Ardent Lilly. Does this facility have an altar?"

"Of course. In the center of the second floor directly above the symbol. I'll begin the alterations while you pray. The others are out raiding, but they should be back before too long."

"Good."

It seemed Durok wanted to make up for his earlier mistake. That pleased her. Not as much as seeing the hero's bloody corpse would please her, but one thing at a time.

CHAPTER 25

Danny dozed in a pew in the Crystal Cathedral. He, along with the girls and a still-sleeping Lyra, were the only ones here at the moment. Eve and the royals had gone to Branik's temple to hand out bread. Eve's magic was needed, but Danny was pretty sure Florian was going so the people would see him helping out. The future king was trying to build up some goodwill with his subjects. Smart and surprising given what Danny had seen during their earlier encounters.

It was a relief that the princesses had gone as well. For the last day, Claudette had been eyeing him with a hungry look. Knowing her proclivities, Danny had no interest in being left alone with her. Not at the moment at least. If he ever got the contraception thing figured out, he'd happily reconsider.

After three meals that consisted of Eve's magic bread and the jerky he had in storage, Danny was ready to go fight demons as long as it got him out of the city. Before they raided the processing facility, he intended to stop at a village inn and eat a proper meal.

A faint squeak drew his attention to the door that led to the back of the cathedral. Lyra emerged a moment later with the girls beside her. Her eyes had their usual golden glow and her dark hair looked freshly combed. All in all she appeared well rested.

Must be nice. Danny hadn't dared sleep deeply given the security situation. A few naps here and there weren't the same. It was lucky for him that his new body was young and resilient.

"Good morning," Danny said. "You look ready to fight a demon horde."

"I feel much better." Lyra looked around. "Where is everyone?"

"The prisoners are locked up and everyone else is handing out magic bread. I assume our next move is to attack the processing facility."

"You assume correctly. Until the priestess is dealt with, the barrier won't come down. How soon can you be ready to leave?"

Danny hopped to his feet. "I'm ready now. Do you want to talk to the imposters again before we go?"

Lyra shrugged. "Do you think they have anything else useful to say?"

"I doubt it. From the sounds of it Richard hadn't visited personally, he just got a few details from the priestess. At a minimum, we should swing by the temple of Branik and say goodbye to Eve. I'd hate for her to come back and find us gone."

"Do you have to leave already, Grandma?" Tara asked.

"Sorry, dearheart, but if we don't bring down the barrier, many innocent people are going to die. Every moment we linger may cost us. Though I'd like nothing better than to stay with you two, my duty is clear."

They hugged her legs and Lyra stroked their hair. To their credit, neither of the girls cried. They were tough kids no doubt about it.

After a final hug, Lyra strode toward the door. Danny waved to the girls and hurried after her. Once they were outside he asked, "Do you think the two of us will be enough?"

"Do you have an alternative? The army has been destroyed and the royal guards co-opted. We're all that's left."

"What about the Golden Claws?"

Lyra made a face. She really didn't like adventurers. "The group has proven themselves useful and loyal. I give them credit for that, but if we take them with us, no one will remain to keep the peace should something happen."

She had a point and, without magical weapons, the adventurers would be of little use against demons. It wasn't like Danny or Lyra was going to be in any position to protect them if this went sideways. Probably better for everyone if they only had themselves to worry about.

He made no more comments as they walked into the courtyard in the center of the temple district. A line of several hundred people stood in front of the temple of Branik. They all stood with their heads hanging down, staring at their feet. They shuffled forward and a moment later a man clutching a loaf of brown bread like it was a sack of gold hurried past.

Lyra ignored them all and went straight to the tables someone had set up in front of the temple. Two of the Golden Claws were standing at either end along with four armed men in heavy mail covered with tabards that sported the inverted sword. Florian stood in the center handing out loaves. There was no sign of Eve.

One of the adventurers motioned them off to one side. "If

you're looking for Lady Carre, she's inside with the other high-ranking priests conjuring bread. If I hadn't seen it with my own eyes I wouldn't have believed it. There's this golden light then poof, a dozen loaves of bread."

He sounded awestruck, which Danny understood. Creation magic was generally considered a miracle, one that seldom happened. Wizards couldn't do it, only high-ranking priests.

"We need to talk to her," Danny said. "Can we go in?"

His gaze shifted to Lyra and he quickly nodded. "Sure. Try not to be too long. We're not even halfway through the breakfast line."

As they headed for the temple door Danny couldn't help smirking. "They really are terrified of you. It would be more amusing if it weren't so sad. What did you do to make people so wary?"

"I've lived for fifteen hundred years and fought in more wars than I care to count. Is that not enough?" Lyra pulled the door open and marched through.

"When you put it that way, I guess it is."

In the center of the chapel, the pews had been pushed aside and several large tables put in their place. Eve, along with five priests Danny didn't recognize, stood around it, their eyes closed and hands raised to the heavens in supplication. As they watched, a golden light appeared and when it faded, twenty loaves of bread covered the table. Several attendants gathered the bread in baskets and hurried past Danny and Lyra.

Eve looked their way and Danny waved. She gave a weary wave in return then pointed off to the side. The trio met up twenty yards from the bread table. Before they could speak Eve hugged Lyra.

The grimace on Lyra's face would bring Danny great joy for the rest of his life.

When she finally let go Eve said, "I was so worried about you. Are you feeling better?"

"Much," Lyra said. "We wanted to stop and let you know we're headed for the demon processing facility. I suspect that, one way or the other, this will be settled within a couple of weeks. If the dome vanishes, you'll know we won. If it doesn't—"

"It will! And you'll both come back safe and sound. Do you want a loaf to take with you?"

"No, thanks," Danny said, perhaps a bit too quickly. "We'll stop and eat at a village on the way. Save your bread for those that truly need it."

Eve smiled. "Then I'll wish you good luck. Adonael watch over you."

Danny didn't trust Adonael much more than Ardent Lilly but he nodded like he appreciated the blessing. "Thanks. See you when we see you."

"I hate to ask," Lyra said. "But will you continue to keep an eye on the girls?"

"Of course," Eve said. "They're really no bother. They play quietly most of the time, though they do enjoy a story before bed."

"Thank you." Lyra bowed before she and Danny headed back out.

They took a different route to the western gate in the hopes of avoiding the crowd. Danny had no idea if she found those people as depressing as he did, but it wouldn't have surprised him.

They hurried through the silent, empty streets. This place would've been just like Forte City minus the demons. He sensed people in the buildings. That was a large improvement.

At the gate they found Guy studying the artifact. The guild master was so close to the hoop that his nose was almost touching it. Somehow Danny imagined bad things would happen if he got any closer.

"You're going to miss breakfast," Danny said.

Guy jumped a foot off the ground then spun to face them. "Ah, I didn't hear you approaching. This is such a fascinating artifact. The more I study it, the more I want to learn all its secrets. As for breakfast, don't worry about me. Eve always saves me a loaf. She's a lovely girl, heaven bless her."

Danny couldn't fault his assessment. "We're going out to find the priestess. I'm not sure if anything will happen when the barrier comes down, but be careful."

"No need to worry. When the power source vanishes, the artifact will return to its original size and fall to the ground. It's perfectly safe."

"That's a relief," Danny said. "How do you know?"

Guy winced. "I don't actually know, but given what I've learned so far about its function, I'm confident in my assessment."

That was less encouraging, but since he'd be hundreds of miles away, Danny decided not to worry about it.

"Has anyone tried to leave?" Lyra asked.

"No. I assumed people would be eager to try their luck in the countryside. Maybe it's the lack of food or some side effect of the barrier, but it seems a certain lethargy has settled over the populace. Hopefully it's a temporary thing."

Danny seconded that. Lyra seemed not to have any more questions so he followed her through the gap. As they jogged down the road Danny said, "I don't know about you, but I'm getting sick of running everywhere."

"Horses would just slow us down and end up as demon food once we got close to the facility."

"Yeah, but it doesn't make me any happier about having to run halfway across the Five Kingdoms for the…third time, I think."

"If it makes you feel better, assuming we survive, we can walk back."

That didn't make Danny feel better at all, but he decided to end the pointless conversation and save his breath for running.

CHAPTER 26

As soon as Durok got started reworking the summoning symbol, Nahia made her way to the altar chamber. It was quite stark, far different from the temple back home. The floor was black tile and the altar itself a dark-gray granite. A crimson cloth embroidered with Ardent Lilly's symbol, a black skull with a lily growing out of its eye, covered most of the stone. A rich aura of darkness filled the space, remnants of the many lives sacrificed.

She breathed deep, letting the corruption fill her body and soul. It felt glorious, nearly as awesome as standing before the portal in Demon King Castle. But she had no time to linger and enjoy the feeling. She strode across the chamber and knelt before the altar, head bowed.

"Mistress, I need your wisdom."

At first nothing happened. A minute passed. Then another. Just when Nahia began to suspect her prayer would go unanswered, she felt a tug and her spirit was yanked from her body. An instant later she stood before a black leather couch upon which reclined the most beautiful being in all existence. Naked as a newborn and blessed with mouthwatering curves, the Lady of Lust was a sight to behold.

Her first words, however, quenched Nahia's lust in an instant. "Your efforts have been a disappointment. You're going to fail and set the mission back. My chosen and I counted on you to prepare the way for her return and you've failed at everything."

Nahia flinched as if her mistress had struck her. To hear such words from the one she loved most hurt. She debated making excuses, but dismissed the idea at once.

"I still have a chance, Mistress. If I sacrifice the lives of all the prisoners we have, I can summon a demon so powerful the hero won't be able to defeat it."

"Stupid wretch." Ardent Lilly spat the words. "You can't summon a demon more powerful than the demon king without a sacrifice many times larger than what you have. How can anything less have any hope of victory?"

"The hero has only one ally and he's been running and fighting for weeks on end. He has to be at the end of his resources. The demon king fought him at full strength. I won't be. Please, Mistress, grant me a powerful champion. Together we can defeat the hero and repair the damage he's done."

Ardent Lilly's glowing red eyes narrowed and for a moment Nahia feared she might be blasted out of existence. "Though I think it likely a waste of resources, I can't simply let you fail, much as you deserve to. Too much is on the line. Return and offer your sacrifice. I will create a champion for you."

Nahia touched her forehead to the floor. "Thank you, Mistress."

When she looked up, she had returned to the altar chamber. Nahia swallowed hard. That had gone about as well as she'd dared to hope. It was also clear to her that, should she fail again, her ultimate fate wouldn't be a pleasant one.

◊

Running, running, and more running. It seemed to be Danny's fate. But at last they were getting close to their target. At least he hoped they were. Otherwise he didn't know what the massive source of corruption about five miles ahead of them might be.

He and Lyra were catching their breath under some maple trees. Two days ago he'd insisted on stopping at a village for a proper meal and to his surprise she hadn't objected. The stew had been wonderful and he ate two bowls, skipping the bread since it reminded him too much of Villipan City. That had been the last village they passed with a living populace. If they failed, those people would likely either be on the run or captured before much longer.

Kind of gave the mission a bit of extra urgency.

"We should put your armor on now, while we have time," Lyra said.

Danny didn't argue. Given what they were likely facing, he'd take every advantage available and to hell with his distaste for all things related to the hero.

As they worked Danny asked, "What do you think we're going to run into?"

"Lots of demons and a few priests. Maybe some undead and ogres thrown in for good measure. Move your right arm."

He obliged and she tightened a strap. "You should keep your distance until I thin them out a bit. Do you want the ethersword?"

She straightened and looked him in the eye. "You trust me to take it?"

"For as long as our interests align I do. You know as well as I do that no one will be safe until these lunatics are dealt with once and for all. When the fight's over, you'd best keep your distance and the sword deactivated."

She shook her head and got to work on his greaves. "You don't have to worry about me. Richard's dead and Florian's a weak boy with more problems than he knows what to do with. No one will be threatening my people anytime soon. As far as I can tell, they all genuinely think you're still dead."

"Leo suspects something. I don't have the right deference to nobility that natives to this world do. I think I've convinced him I'm an on-the-run nobleman. With any luck I'll be long gone before anyone figures out the truth."

She straightened and handed him the helmet, accepting the ethersword in exchange. "I won't be pleased to see you leave, but it will mean we've won, so I won't complain."

Lyra could complain until she was blue in the face; it wouldn't make any difference to his plans. "Let's go."

They marched forward at a steady walk. There was no need to rush now. Danny had no desire to arrive out of breath. They'd timed their assault for noon. Mostly for symbolic reasons rather than because it made any difference in the enemy's strength.

Marching into a battle to the death on a bright, sunny day seemed wrong. A memory of the last picnic he took Suzy on popped unbidden into Danny's mind. The weather had been about the same as this and he'd been on a ten-day leave. That happened, what, six months before he was brought to this world? It was a good day, just the two of them sitting by a brook, talking about the future while eating ham-and-cheese sandwiches.

They'd made so many plans, all of which died with Danny's old body. He snarled and forced the memories away. They were too painful and he had demons to kill.

At the top of a small hill Danny froze. A massive, crude fortress rose out of the plains in front of them. If Danny had harbored any doubt that it was the source of the corruption they'd been following, the army of several thousand thralls would've confirmed the truth.

"I'm not sure what I expected, but this wasn't it," Danny said.

"They must've started construction almost immediately after the demon king was defeated," Lyra said. "We're going to have to force our way through."

"I've been thinking about a new spell," Danny said. "This is the perfect chance to try it."

"Are you sure? Maybe sticking with tried-and-true magic would be best under the circumstances."

"I'm sure."

Danny hadn't been the biggest anime fan back home, but he did watch it now and then with his little brother. There was one thing he'd always wanted to try and now that he was in a fantasy world, he could.

Holding his gauntleted hands about a foot apart, Danny ran ether through the mithril then gathered it into a ball. He pictured the ball turning white as it transformed into holy energy. The power gradually grew denser until he could barely contain it.

He threw his hands forward and shouted, "Ha!"

A beam of white light shot out at the thrall army. When it hit in the center of their formation, an explosion of holy energy shot out in every direction.

The light faded, revealing a fifty-foot circle now free of thralls.

Grinning, Danny said, "That worked better than I'd hoped."

"I've never seen a spell like that. What do you call it?"

"Holy Spirit Wave. Come on, let's finish them off before they recover." Danny drew the hero's sword and charged.

He managed five strides before a pillar of darkness nearly as big around as the fortress exploded into the sky.

◐

Nahia's face twisted in concentration as she reworked a section of the summoning circle. She and Durok were nearly done and a good thing too. She'd sensed a large quantity of mithril getting closer by the moment. That could only mean one thing. The hero was coming. Despite working without sleep since she finished speaking with Ardent Lilly, they still hadn't been able to finish. She couldn't even blame anyone, much as she wished it were otherwise. Changing the function of such a large circle simply took time. And, while Nahia had some things in abundance, time wasn't one of them.

"Finished," Durok said.

She let slip a little hiss of annoyance. The miserable wretch shouldn't have finished before she did. Ignoring his smug tone, she shifted an ethereal line and fused it to another.

Almost finished.

"Fetch the prisoners. I'll be done in thirty seconds."

She was vaguely aware of his footsteps receding. Two more connections. The ether shifted at her mental command.

Sweat blurred her vision.

Nahia blinked it away and kept going.

One more connection.

An explosion of holy energy ripped through the corruption that infused the building. Hundreds of thralls dying at once nearly overwhelmed her senses. Gritting her teeth so hard her jaw ached, she focused through the chaos.

Come on, align!

There! The final connection was complete and not a moment too soon. She straightened in time to watch Durok and the three succubi herding scores of dazed humans into the courtyard.

Nahia sprinted clear of the circle as the sacrifices streamed in. The source of the mithril was getting closer all the time.

It was only a few yards away when the last man entered the circle. "Mistress, accept this sacrifice and send your champion to our aid."

Nahia trigged the circle and felt all the sacrifices' lives get snuffed out in an instant. A black pillar shot into the air. When it faded, a beautiful woman stood in the center of the circle. Her skin was pale, her hair dark, and eyes red. She looked, in fact, exactly like Ardent Lilly herself.

When she understood what the new arrival was, Nahia hit her knees and touched her head to the ground. "Welcome, Mistress. Thank you for coming to our aid."

The avatar of Ardent Lilly spoke with a throaty purr that would turn men's heart to mush. "The hero is close, I can feel his presence."

"Yes, Mistress. We barely completed the summoning in time."

"Rise and look at me."

Nahia obeyed, scrambling to her feet and looking into the burning red eyes.

"Pathetic though you are, your efforts are not without

merit. Once I've dealt with the hero, we will return to the city together. When the demon king returns, we shall welcome her and celebrate as she destroys the hated cathedral that we might rule this world without Heaven's interference."

"As you say, Mistress." Nahia hoped it went as the avatar said, but her doubts refused to be quieted.

The gate exploded inward and a figure decked from head to toe in silver armor strode through. He held a silver sword in his hands and looked from Nahia to the avatar and back.

"I don't suppose you'd like to surrender and lower the barrier around Villipan City?" he asked.

The avatar laughed.

"I thought not, but figured it couldn't hurt to ask." The hero sounded genuinely disappointed.

"Fall back," the avatar said. "This is my fight."

Nahia didn't even think to argue as she fled for the stairs to the second floor. Durok fell in beside her along with the demons. Whatever happened, their part was finished.

CHAPTER 27

Danny stood facing the most beautiful female he'd ever seen. All her bits were perfect, almost too perfect. She looked more like an illustration brought to life than a real person. Appropriate, given that she was a demon. A powerful one at that if the surge of corruption he'd felt earlier was any indication.

Something powerful tugged at his mind, but his antipsychic magic spell held. Danny kept it running constantly. He'd encountered so many things capable of controlling his thoughts that doing otherwise would've been stupid. The spell didn't drain him enough to say so.

"I hadn't thought to meet you face to face, Hero," the demon said.

"Why would you? I've run into plenty of demons, but I don't go out of my way to do so. They all keep trying to kill me."

"That's hardly fair," the demon said. "Didn't my priestesses offer you the chance to join our side?"

Danny frowned. "Your priestesses? You can't be a demon

lord. I might not know a lot about summoning, but it would take a lot more than this to bring one to the real world."

"You're quite right. I'm an avatar, the very tiniest sliver of Ardent Lilly's consciousness. You should be honored that my minions had to resort to summoning me. Not just anyone is worthy of my personal attention."

"I'm not sure honored is the right word," Danny said. "Was there anything else you wanted to discuss or shall we begin?"

"Don't be so hasty." She leaned forward and her breasts swayed from side to side. "I want to give you one more chance to join me. It's not too late. When my demon king returns, you two can rule the world together. With your combined might, nothing could stop you."

The pull on Danny's mind grew stronger, but his protective magic held. "Still not interested. And this whole trying to control my mind thing isn't going to work. You're stronger than the succubus that tried it before, but not nearly strong enough."

A black sword appeared out of nowhere and the avatar raised it to high guard. "So be it. When you die screaming and vomiting blood, don't say I didn't give you the chance to join the winning side."

Where did they come up with these lines?

Danny tightened his grip on the hero's sword. "I promise I won't."

He kicked the ground hard enough to crack the earth and closed the distance between himself and the demon in an instant. Despite his speed, she parried the first slash easily. The black sword turned aside his mithril blade, but Danny wasn't shocked.

Slashing and stabbing, he kept up the pressure.

His opponent seemed to float around, effortlessly

dodging or redirecting his strikes. She was nearly as fast and considerably more skilled than the demon king.

Danny blew out a breath and stopped. Chasing this thing around wasn't doing him any good. He needed a new strategy.

"Giving up already?" the avatar asked.

Danny ignored her and sent ether rushing through his armor, purifying the corruption. When he had enough, he pushed outward, forming a bubble. Foot by foot, he expanded it.

Soon he felt the avatar back away. She slashed her sword through the bubble, but Danny repaired it instantly. Painstakingly he kept increasing the diameter. It wouldn't be long now.

When he sensed the avatar's back was to the wall, he gathered himself and sprang forward.

Danny emerged from the light right in front of her and slashed hard.

Somehow she got an arm up to block.

Danny sliced it off at the elbow. Forearm and black sword both fell to the floor and vanished in a puff of black smoke.

The avatar hissed in pain.

No way was he going to give her a chance to recover. Danny kept his assault going, slicing little bits of darkness away with each swing. By some miracle she kept just enough ahead of him to avoid a fatal blow. Between conjuring the bubble and maintaining his physical enhancements, Danny was getting worn out. He needed to end this fight soon.

The question was how? He wasn't exactly holding back.

The avatar leapt away. Her body was bleeding black blood from numerous wounds and her body slumped. Clearly Danny wasn't the only one in rough condition. He found that heartening.

"Miserable wretch! How dare you treat a near goddess this way?"

Danny was happy to catch his breath for a moment. "This is how fights work. I try to kill you and you try to kill me. The winner is the one who doesn't die. For a so-called goddess, you're not very bright."

Her eyes flashed brighter. So, she didn't like being insulted. Maybe he could use that to his advantage.

"I have to say, I'm really disappointed. When you told me you were an avatar of a demon lord I had much higher expectations. All you've been able to do is run away. Even your sad excuse for a demon king did better than you. She left me battered and bruised to the point of collapse. All you can manage is a bit of light cardio."

"I'm going to shove those words down your throat and rip your heart out."

"Yeah, yeah. I hear a lot of talk, but I'm not seeing much action. What, are you hoping I'll die of boredom?"

He could almost hear her teeth grinding.

The only warning he got was a faint tensing of her muscles.

She sprang at him, quick as a bullet, clawed hand leading.

Danny dodged right and slashed.

She twisted out of the way, her body contorting in a way no human's could.

Before he had a chance to recover, her claws scraped across the back of his armor. They didn't do any damage, but he did stagger forward. Using his momentum, Danny tucked and rolled back up to his feet.

Just in time to find the avatar in his face.

Her fist crashed into his helmet and sent him flying across the room. He bounced, skidded, and finally slammed against the wall.

"Shit." Maybe pissing her off wasn't the best strategy.

Danny rolled over. As soon as his back hit the ground the avatar pinned him down, her knees, protected by a dark aura, holding his shoulders so he couldn't move his arms.

He looked up at her twisted, enraged face. "You know, if you keep making that expression, your face might freeze that way."

She screamed and reached for his helmet. As soon as her bare hands touched the mithril she jerked back.

That shifted her weight just enough. With a wrench he yanked his arms free and wrapped them around her waist. Once he had a hold of her, Danny channeled every drop of holy energy he could conjure through his armor.

White light exploded out and when it did, the avatar's screams doubled and then doubled again, rising to a crescendo that hurt Danny's ears. The holy energy burned her corrupt essence away until nothing remained.

Danny blew out a long breath and tried to stand. His body declined in no uncertain terms. Lyra would have to deal with the priestess on her own. That fight had been as difficult in its own way as battling the demon king. With any luck, he wouldn't have to do it again anytime soon.

○

Lyra wrapped herself in invisibility and waited. Through the ruined door she could see Daniel talking with a beautiful female demon. There was no sign of the priestess, but she assumed the woman had fled to the second floor. No one in their right mind would want to get between the hero and a demon as powerful as this one. And while she had her doubts about any demon worshipper being in their right mind, their survival instinct was beyond question. She just needed Daniel to keep the demon busy while she snuck past and dealt with the humans and any remaining demons.

Why was he even talking to that thing? All a demon would do was lie and twist your words to its own ends. They should be killed on sight. At least she thought so. Lyra had serious doubts Daniel would be interested in her opinions. She'd burned that bridge to ash.

The first blow came so fast, she didn't see either of them move. Only the explosion of sound as their weapons clashed signaled the start of the battle.

Lyra slipped into the massive room and worked her way around the outer wall. Daniel and his opponent were moving so fast she could barely see them. Trying her best to stay out of the way, she moved as quickly as stealth would allow toward the steps up to the second floor. Lucky for her the fight had moved to the far side of the room as she climbed.

At the top she found the door unprotected. Staying to one side, she poked it open. Nothing appeared to attack her. Peeking around the frame, she found the area clear and lit by glowing red crystals spaced every ten yards or so. They gave everything an eerie glow that made her a bit queasy. While far from interested in looks herself, she couldn't deny her disgust at the cultists' taste in decorations. It's like they wanted everything covered in blood.

Shaking her head, Lyra ended her invisibility spell and lit the ethersword. It felt good to carry a weapon that had been used by the greatest heroes of her people. The hilt fit her hand perfectly, like it was made for her.

The hall beyond the door branched left and right. With no better options she went right. She listened hard as she walked. Trying to sense the priestess's corruption was a wasted effort in this place. Only something as powerful as the demon below would stand out against the building's aura.

It didn't take long to reach the first door. She heard nothing, but kicked it open to make sure. Inside was a basic bedroom smaller than the one the girls shared at the mansion. It pleased her for some reason that these maniacs weren't living in luxury. The next three rooms were also bedrooms. It seemed she'd chosen to investigate the building's dormitory.

The hall ended in a blank wall, forcing her to backtrack. If nothing else she knew where the priestess wasn't.

She turned around and nearly ran into the bare chest of the priest from Forte. She'd heard and seen nothing. How had he taken her so completely off guard?

A powerful backhanded blow sent her flying into the wall.

By some miracle she kept a grip on the ethersword.

Scrambling to her feet, she angled her weapon and crouched, ready for the next attack.

Instead he smiled at her. "I feared we might not get to meet. We were so close in Forte. If your friend hadn't interfered we could've had so much fun. You wouldn't believe the things we learn as followers of the Lady of Lust."

"I'd sooner sleep with a crimson ogre."

His smile widened and twisted into something crueler. "I can arrange that. And if it's the worst thing I do to you for the humiliation of driving me out of my own city, consider yourself fortunate. The hero won't be able to save you this time. The avatar will end him."

That demon was an avatar of Ardent Lilly? She was surprised, but still felt confident Daniel could handle it.

"If you come quiet—"

Lyra launched herself at the priest, ethersword cutting down at his right shoulder.

He leapt back, evading the blow. Darkness gathered around his fists as he raised them to a ready position. Did he think he could beat her barehanded?

She thrust at his chest.

He spun around the blade, dodging by such a small fraction that his robe ended up sliced.

A black-clad fist came crashing in at her head.

Lyra ducked and slashed, planning to take it off at the wrist. Her blade hit the dark aura, pushing his hand away but not cutting through.

They faced off again. The priest had lost his smile, which pleased her more than it should've.

"You're stronger than I thought. It seems you're not the Champion of Villipan for nothing."

Lyra stayed silent and ready. She wasn't the type to chat. As soon as he showed her an opening, she planned to drive her sword through it.

Unfortunately, he didn't offer any openings. His black-clad hands stayed close to his chest, protecting his vitals. He might be an arrogant loudmouth, but he knew how to fight.

"Nothing to say?" he asked. "No insults or witty remarks? A one-sided conversation isn't very interesting."

Lyra still didn't speak. Instead she gathered holy energy in the hilt of the ethersword before launching a white lance at the priest.

He slapped it aside, making a small gap in his defenses.

She lunged.

He twisted away. A flick of her wrist cut a long groove in his side, drawing a pained hiss. It took no effort to cut with the ethersword; that's what made it so dangerous.

"Bitch! I'll kill you for that."

He charged in, fists leading. Despite his anger, the technique behind the strikes remained excellent. Even with her physical enhancements, it took all she had to avoid them. Lyra didn't know what would happen if one of those black-clad fists made contact with her and she wasn't keen on finding out.

Though her blade couldn't cut through his hands, it did allow her to parry with no issue. So they danced around, each looking for an opening and neither finding one. That was okay with Lyra. The longer the fight went, the better the chances Daniel would finish his fight and come to lend a hand.

Her opponent, on the other hand, assuming his scowling, grim expression was any indication, was getting frustrated. Good, frustrated people often made mistakes.

As she'd hoped, moment by moment his movements grew more erratic and desperate. Perhaps he'd never had to fight someone capable of lasting this long.

Finally he overextended on a right cross.

Lyra didn't hesitate. A hard slash with the ethersword took his arm off at the elbow. When he screamed, she thrust the blade through his mouth and out the back of his skull. He collapsed and didn't move. Just to be sure, Lyra sliced his head off.

When she was sure the priest was dead, Lyra blew out a sigh. That fight had been far closer than she'd expected. And she was pretty sure he was subordinate to the priestess who captured her in Villipan City. If she was right, she had an even tougher fight waiting for her.

CHAPTER 28

Nahia sensed it when Durok died. It didn't surprise her. When she sent the fool to deal with the elf-blood woman, Lyra—unless she was mistaken—who thought herself sneaky, Nahia had expected him to die. It would've been nice if he'd taken the annoying woman with him, but, as had become abundantly clear, Nahia's fondest desires were not being granted at the moment.

She'd briefly considered making a run for it, but since she couldn't leave the circle created by the hell portals, there seemed little point. Better to face her fate here, where she was at her strongest.

And so she sat on the altar, the three surviving succubi at her side, and waited to see who would show up to try and kill her. She hoped it would be Lyra. Nahia wanted to see *her* dead even more than the hero.

Nahia clutched her chest and gasped.

"Mistress?" one of the succubi asked.

Nahia waved her off. This wasn't her pain, but the psychic backlash of Ardent Lilly's avatar dying. The hero had defeated her. Much like with Durok's defeat, she wasn't shocked. Despite all the life force they'd sacrificed, the avatar wasn't as strong as the demon king and the corruption here was weaker than Demon King Castle. The odds of victory had always been long.

"What should we do?" a second succubus asked, a tremor of fear in her sultry voice.

"We wait and see who we need to fight first," Nahia said. "Victory or death is all that awaits us."

She hated how fatalistic she sounded, but the truth was the truth. Their position was terrible and their options nonexistent. Not exactly where Nahia hoped to find herself at this point in the mission, but here she was.

About ten minutes after Durok's death, Nahia sensed a small quantity of mithril approaching. That would be Lyra, good. The hero still shone like a second sun on the ground floor. Since he hadn't moved, she assumed the avatar had taken more out of him than Nahia had feared. Four on one, she might have a chance of winning the first round.

Eventually the door opened and the elf-blood appeared, holding a blade of glowing white energy. Nahia had never seen an ethersword before, but she'd read about them in ancient texts. The weapons were nearly as destructive as mithril blades.

Nahia unclipped her whip from her belt and hopped off the altar. The succubi spread out left and right, ready to attack from the flanks should an opening present itself. A flick of her wrist made the whip crack and burn with hellfire.

The elf-blood stalked silently forward, her face a mask of grim determination.

Nahia considered a bit of taunting, but doubted her opponent would be so easily distracted.

A second snap of her wrist sent a ball of hellfire blazing in.

Lyra dodged left and sprinted toward the nearest succubus at blinding speed. A single slash cut the demon in half. She instantly started to dissolve.

The other two hissed and charged, seeming enraged by the loss of their sister. Nahia covered their approach with more hellfire blasts. In the end, two demons fared no better than one and it was only Nahia and Lyra standing in the altar chamber.

"No more lackeys to send after me?" Lyra asked.

Nahia shook her head. If she'd had any more lackeys, she would've happily sent them, but she was on her own now.

"I usually dislike killing, necessary though it is, but you threatened my granddaughters. For that, I will enjoy sending your soul to meet your master."

"You will try." Nahia set her whip spinning in a figure-eight pattern, making a wall of hellfire between herself and Lyra.

A lance of holy energy shot in only to be burned away when it hit the flames.

Nahia countered with black beams of her own, but they were cut down as soon as they got close. It was a standoff and whoever ran out of strength first would die.

Lyra glared at the priestess through the tiny gaps in the hellfire wall. She wanted nothing so much as to end this and return home. But she saw no opening in the woman's defense. Daniel clearly wasn't coming to her aid. She'd sensed the avatar die, but the battle must've wearied him. Either that or he was hoping the priestess would kill her.

No, she wasn't being fair. Daniel was a good man. And if he wanted her dead, he was more than strong enough to do the job himself.

A lance of black energy shot out. Lyra sliced it in half.

Right, focus. She had to assume that she was on her own and act accordingly. First up was finding a way to reach her opponent. Waiting her out was an option. Maintaining the wall had to be taking a toll. If Lyra was patient, her opponent might collapse from exhaustion. Finishing her then would be a simple matter.

More dark lances streaked out, slower and weaker than before. Lyra evaded them easily. Yes, the priestess was definitely getting weaker. Soon enough her patience would be rewarded.

Lyra wasn't the only one who realized it either. The hellfire wall shifted, growing and flowing around her before starting to close in.

So much for waiting.

Lyra channeled power through the hilt then formed it into a protective bubble. Sprinting forward, she leapt through the flames, choking off a scream as she did. Even with her barrier spell in place, the corrupt fire burned her.

Emerging from the flames, Lyra thrust where she expected to find the priestess waiting. And instead found empty air.

Something wrapped around her, burning her arms and torso before lifting her off her feet and slamming her into the wall with bone-shattering force. Her shield kept the damage to a minimum but the air was still knocked out of her.

Gasping for breath, she struggled to her feet only to get kicked back to the floor.

Lyra looked up to find the priestess towering over her. "I may not be strong enough to defeat the hero, but at least I'll die knowing I sent you to whatever hell claims you."

Pain, fear, and anger combined to drive Lyra into motion.

The priestess's whip came down, missing her by inches. Hellfire licked her back, but at this point, the extra pain barely registered.

Gathering herself, Lyra lunged, driving the ethersword through the priestess's chest.

She dropped her whip and a little smile formed on her blood-flecked lips. "It seems I underestimated you. Again."

After breathing out those final words, the woman collapsed. With the last of her strength, Lyra sliced the corpse's head off.

The pain she'd blocked off came roaring back and with a final moan, Lyra collapsed.

CHAPTER 29

Danny's strength slowly returned as he lay on the floor and stared at the plain gray ceiling. He wasn't sure how long had passed since his fight with Ardent Lilly's avatar ended, but it seemed like long enough that Lyra should've finished up her business and rejoined him or, if she lost, the priestess should've come to finish him off. Adding to his confusion were the hundreds of thralls milling around outside and not trying to kill him. In Danny's experience, trying to kill him was a thrall's favorite pastime.

He sighed, tried to sit up, and succeeded. That was a step in the right direction. Next he forced himself to his feet and smiled at the minimal wobble in his knees. Finally he collected the hero's sword and set off for the steps at a determined shuffle. After a few strides his pace increased. Everything hurt, but he was pretty sure he hadn't been injured. When you were a soldier, you learned the difference in a hurry.

Taking the steps one at a time like a three-year-old,

Danny was glad no one was around to see his pitiful display. Still, he was moving and getting stronger by the moment. He might be up to fighting a single zombie in a few minutes.

Pausing at the top of the stairs, he looked left and right. There were no clues as to which way she went and he couldn't sense anything in this corrupt place.

"Lyra!" he shouted.

No reply.

"Hey, if you're still alive, say something!"

Still no reply.

"Well, shit."

With a shrug he turned right and walked at a reasonably normal pace down the eerie crimson hall. Danny didn't know if haunted houses were a thing in this world, but if they were he was going to hire a demon cult to build one for him. They had the aesthetic down to a T.

At the end of the hall he found a man's headless corpse. He was pretty sure it was the priest from Forte. Looked like Lyra had already been here and gone.

Retracing his steps, Danny tried the left-hand passage. This one led to a large room with an altar in the center. Lyra lay unmoving on the floor not far from a dead woman Danny assumed was the priestess they'd been hunting.

He hurried to Lyra and knelt beside her. Taking his gauntlet off, he touched his fingers to the side of her neck. Between his weakness and the background corruption, he couldn't sense her life force. When he found a strong pulse he relaxed a bit. Her body was covered with nasty burn marks and the side of her face was a mass of bruises. She'd won, but paid a high price for it.

Trying to heal her here would be a fool's errand. They needed to leave this corrupted place. Assuming the thralls would let them leave, of course. Cutting his way out, in his current condition while protecting Lyra would be a big ask. Maybe an impossible one.

Wait, cutting his way out didn't have to mean through the thralls. He could hack an opening out of the rear of the building and sneak away. Hopefully.

The ethersword sat on the ground a few feet from Lyra. He put it into storage before lifting her off the floor and into his arms. How could someone so skinny be so heavy? With a little shake of his head, Danny retraced his steps to the first floor. He set Lyra down and drew his sword.

Taking a breath to steady himself, he thrust the mithril sword into the stone wall. It was like cutting pudding. Even rock posed no obstacle for the hero's sword. Dragging it around, he cut a crude circle then pulled the sword free. A few more slices carved the disk into chunks small enough that he could push them out of the way. Danny was forced to use a bit of physical enhancement but at last he had an opening big enough for them to pass through.

With Lyra in his arms, he walked away from the processing facility as quickly as his weary legs would allow. Some cleanup work remained to be done, but it felt like they'd won the big battle.

At least Danny hoped they had.

○

Lyra's eyes flickered open as a comforting warmth wrapped her body. A few blinks cleared her vision enough to reveal a clearing surrounded by trees. The worst of her pains were gone. She rolled over to find Daniel kneeling beside her, his hands glowing white. He was still dressed in the hero's armor, though the helmet lay off to one side.

"Stop moving around, I wasn't finished healing the other side."

She moved back to her original position and asked, "What happened?"

"We won. The bad guys, or maybe I should say gals since two of them were female, are dead. I carried you here once my strength returned and got busy healing. Those burns are stubborn, but I'm almost done."

"Wounds caused by hellfire always heal slowly. I didn't expect to wake up again."

"Yeah, you were in rough shape. Okay, all done." She sat up and Daniel dropped to the ground beside her. "I'm pretty well beat."

"Why did you save me?"

"I've got two reasons and you know them both already."

Lyra shook her head. "There has to be more to it. I know you're fond of the girls and don't want to see them cry, but if I'd died in battle, they wouldn't have blamed you."

Daniel looked her in the eye, all signs of joking gone. "We were on the same team. When you go into a fight, you watch your teammate's back. You patch them up when they get hurt. If you have to, you carry them on your back to safety. I'd have done the same for any of my guys back home and a few of them were real assholes, though to be fair none of them killed me. You're also my backup plan."

Lyra cocked her head. "Backup plan?"

"Yeah. If I can't figure out how to sever the link between this world and mine, eventually another hero will be summoned. Much as I hate the idea, having you here to train him, give him the armor and sword, and hopefully not murder him should he win, will ensure he has the best chance of surviving a bad situation."

Lyra scrubbed a hand across her face and rubbed her eyes. "You've thought a lot about this."

"I have. My responsibilities are clear and I take them seriously. I have to do this right."

She offered a slow, sad smile. "This is what makes you so different from the other heroes. They were all good boys who wanted to do the right thing, but they didn't really understand what the right thing was or how difficult it could be to figure out which right thing you needed to do."

"Comparing my situation to theirs is unfair. Before I came here, I'd traveled the world, killed men, and seen friends die. Three years in the Marines might as well be a lifetime. Comparing me to some kid still in high school is like comparing a pet dog to a trained war hound. Anyway, if you're up to it, I'd appreciate your help getting out of this armor."

"You still trust me now that the fighting is over?"

He showed no sign of smiling. "Before I healed you, I checked you for weapons. Unless you think you can take me with your bare hands while I'm alert to the danger, I think I'll be okay."

She swallowed a sigh as they stood. It seemed he really was never going to trust her again. Not that she could fault him for the decision.

Lyra got busy unbuckling straps. Once the greaves were off she said, "I think it would be best to rest until morning before we return to Villipan City."

"I have no intention of going anywhere today. As for the city, I'm not going back. You can sign my contract then we'll part ways. Say goodbye to Eve and the girls for me."

She paused halfway through unbuckling his breastplate. "What do you mean you're not going back? The Five Kingdoms are still in chaos. We could use your help straightening things out."

"The city should be free and frankly I've done all I care to. Fall is here. I may have missed the grand caravan already, but I figure on my own I won't have much trouble catching up. You, Eve, and whoever else you can find to help will have to fix the rest."

Lyra hadn't wanted to believe Daniel was going to leave despite what he'd said. Foolish of her, in retrospect. She got busy removing the rest of the hero's armor. When she'd returned both armor and sword to her pocket dimension, Daniel stretched and gave a full-body shake.

"That armor is great to wear in a fight, but it gets hot in a hurry." He let out a huge yawn. "I know it's early, but I'm beat. Oh, before I forget."

He opened his own pocket dimension and pulled out their contract, along with a quill and ink. "I'd say I lived up to the terms and then some."

Lyra took the paper and conjured a flat surface to write on. "You certainly have. Villipan owes you a debt it can never repay and not just for the last few weeks. On a personal note, I'm very grateful for all you did for both myself and the girls despite having no reason in the world to go out of your way to help us."

"You're welcome." He took back the pen and paper and put them away. "Sleep well."

Daniel moved about ten yards away before conjuring an anti-corruption barrier around their camp. Next he lay down and made a second, smaller barrier around himself. Just a reminder of where she stood.

Lyra sighed, feeling all of her fifteen hundred years. Hopefully things would look better in the morning.

CHAPTER 30

Danny woke in the predawn gloom. The air had a chill. Fall was here and no mistake. He was beyond ready to leave this place behind. He might miss Eve and the girls, maybe even Lyra, at least a little, but that was it. He'd invested far more time in cleaning up their messes than he intended. It was time to get down to his own business.

He sat up, quiet as a mouse, and glanced over at Lyra. As far as he could tell she was sound asleep. Since goodbyes were not his thing, just leaving struck him as an excellent plan. He'd leave the ward in place so nothing would trouble her before she was ready to deal with it. Satisfied with his plan, Danny got to his feet, made a little gap in the ward, and stepped out.

Once he sealed it back up he headed toward the processing facility. It wasn't far out of his way and he wanted to see what the remaining thralls were up to. Just to be safe, he activated his stealth field.

It took twenty minutes to retrace his steps from the day before. It seemed like hours the last time he made the walk. In front of the ruined building he found the thralls standing around staring at nothing. While far from an expert on all things demonic, Danny knew enough to tell their behavior was off. Had the death of their creators done something to them? He'd expected to find them all gone, having wandered off to find some humans to slaughter. Not that there were any nearby.

He shrugged. This was way better.

He retrieved the ethersword from storage and lit it. Using minimal physical enhancement, he charged in.

Six of them lay in pieces before the rest had a chance to react. The mob tried to surround him, but Danny was far too fast. Killing thralls, even this many of them, was no challenge for him. It was more like harvesting wheat with the ether-sword serving as a scythe.

The process took half an hour and when he was done, all the thralls had been destroyed. If Lyra wanted to burn the bodies, that was up to her. None of them had heads anymore, so it should be fine either way.

Job done, he walked through the ruined gate and took a close look at the summoning circle. As far as he could tell it remained intact. That wouldn't do at all. He crisscrossed it several times, letting the ethersword's blade drag along the floor, cutting through carefully laid lines and severing magical connections. By the time he was finished, anyone wanting to use it would have to start from scratch.

Danny couldn't think of anything else to do, so he turned northeast. He wasn't sure exactly where he was, but that general direction should take him to Rosenbar. Despite what he said to Lyra, he wasn't in a huge rush. Having run here and there nonstop for weeks, he planned to enjoy the nice weather and take his time. If he found a village with an extra horse, it wouldn't hurt his feelings to buy a mount.

Smiling to himself, he set out across the fields. It was a good day to be alive and he intended to enjoy it.

B right sunlight dazzled Lyra for a moment when she opened her eyes. Her whole body felt stiff, but there was no real pain, thank heaven for small mercies. When she sat up and looked around she saw no sign of Daniel. True to his word, he'd left already.

But he kept the ward up. Lyra appreciated his consideration.

Getting slowly to her feet, she wondered if she'd ever see him again and suspected the answer was no. He would have to circle the entire continent to destroy the hero summoning spell and she had no idea how long that might take. A lifetime seemed well within the realm of possibility. And even if it didn't take that long, assuming he survived the journey, she doubted Daniel would want to settle in the Five Kingdoms.

She took a drink from her waterskin. No, she was pretty sure she'd never see this cycle's hero again. It was a pity given how much work it was going to be getting Villipan back to something approaching normal, but she accepted it. As always, Lyra would do what she had to in order to keep her people and their new home safe.

And the first thing she needed to do was see how many demons remained to be eliminated. Hopefully she could hire some adventurers to help her wipe out the remaining thralls. She grimaced at the idea of relying on them, but desperate times frequently required desperate measures.

A wave of her hand dispelled Daniel's ward and she set

out, invisible, for the fortress. When she arrived she found freshly killed thralls littering the ground and not a single survivor visible. A quick peek inside the fortress revealed a summoning circle slashed apart and ruined.

A little smile creased her lips. Looked like Daniel had swung by ahead of her. Generous of him and she appreciated it.

Taking a moment to orient herself, Lyra set out for home. If heaven blessed her, she'd find Villipan City barrier free.

CHAPTER 31

Danny walked down the busy streets of Rosenbar. The people were out and about, taking care of their daily business, and acting like they had no idea what had happened in the capital or across the border. And they probably didn't. One of the advantages of no mass communications was that people tended to focus on local problems and didn't worry about the bigger picture. He envied them.

Only the gate guards had been nervous. They were still worried about demons despite the fact that there hadn't been a sighting in weeks. Danny had been tempted to reassure them, but he didn't know for a fact the threat was over. If he said something and turned out to be wrong, well, he didn't want to risk it.

Informing the people about where things stood was Florian's job. Let him send royal messengers.

He eased to one side of the street to let a wagon loaded with barrels trundle by. Turning down a secondary avenue, Danny paused by a stall selling squash. It looked nice and fresh. A middle-aged woman in a tan dress with a red scarf tied around her head looked up at him.

"How's the harvest going?"

"Much better, sir. Summer vegetables and fresh meat have been arriving several times a week. This yellow squash came in just last evening."

"Before I left people were afraid to go beyond the wall."

She nodded. "It was bad for a while, but weeks with no more attacks gave people confidence. It feels like Rosenbar is getting back to normal."

Danny grinned. Back to normal. Those were sweet words indeed.

"Thanks for the chat. Good morning."

He left the stand and continued on his way to the Adventurers' Guild. Danny offered a nod or wave to the people he passed. It was a marked improvement over the capital and he found his spirits buoyed. Coming here and seeing this made it feel like everything he'd gone through had been worth it.

At last, he reached the guild and pushed through the door. Unlike last time he visited, not a soul could be found in the waiting area. Emily and Timothy were at their posts behind the counter. When she spotted him, Emily offered a bright smile. Danny strode over, pulling the signed contract out of his satchel as he got closer.

"I was afraid you wouldn't make it back," she said. "Taking a job with Lady Shael was terribly dangerous."

And Emily didn't know the half of it. "I can't find fault with your observation, but we made it through and finished the job."

He handed over the contract. Emily checked it over then nodded. "Everything looks in order. Your fee's in the safe. I'll go fetch it then I can upgrade your guild card to elite."

"Much obliged."

Emily hurried off toward the guild master's office and the huge iron safe therein. Danny turned around and leaned against the counter. It was strange not having the other adventurers hanging around. He'd been hoping to see the look on Bruno's face when he made it back in one piece. Another disappointment, but a small one.

"Welcome back, Ronin." Danny turned to find Guild Master Duret approaching with a heavy-looking pouch in his hand. "I was worried you wouldn't make it."

"It was rough, no doubt. Lady Shael worked me pretty hard."

Emily ducked back behind the counter. "I'll swap your old card for a new, elite one."

Danny handed it over. "Thanks."

Duret gave him the bag. It had to weigh ten pounds. Much as he wanted to put it into storage at once, he didn't want to answer any questions even more.

"If you want to store some of that in the safe, you're welcome to do so," Duret offered.

"I appreciate the offer, but I hope to leave the Five Kingdoms soon and I'll need traveling funds. That was the whole point of taking the job after all. Don't worry, I'll be careful with it. On another subject, where is everyone?"

"Out on jobs." Duret sounded pleased. "Now that it's clear leaving the city isn't a death sentence, business has picked up. We're not back to peak, but it's enough to keep everyone busy."

"All set." Emily had a new copper badge that looked exactly like his old one.

"Thanks." Danny took it and flipped it over. It was exactly like his old one only it said elite instead of journeyman under his name. He'd kind of hoped for one made of silver or gold, but whatever. He pocketed the badge.

"Still planning to join the grand caravan?" Duret asked.

Danny nodded. "Yup, assuming it hasn't left already. My next stop is to see if they've got a spot for me. I hope to be on the road before much longer. Though if it's going to be more than a week, I might stop back and take a job or two just to kill time."

"You're more than welcome." Duret held out his hand and Danny gave it a shake. "I expect big things from you, Ronin. If you make S-rank I'll be sure to brag that you joined up at my guild."

Danny grinned. "I hope I don't disappoint. Guild Master, Emily, it's been a pleasure. So long."

With a little wave, Danny headed for the door. Once he was outside, he turned toward Trevor's warehouse. He figured the easiest place to find out about the son's caravan was to ask his father.

It wasn't a long walk and soon Danny stood in front of the large single-story structure. The main double doors were open and a wagon was being unloaded by a pair of burly teamsters. Off to one side, Robi was keeping a quiet eye on them.

Danny whistled and when Robi looked his way gave a little wave. Robi grinned back and motioned him over.

They shook hands and Robi said, "Ronin, good to see you again. When you took that job with Lady Shael I feared you wouldn't live through it."

"You and everyone else. It was a tough one," Danny said with total honesty. "I definitely feel like I earned my promotion to elite."

"Congratulations. We'll have to get an ale tonight to celebrate. What brings you by?"

"Trevor mentioned his son was planning a grand caravan. I wanted to see if that was still the case and if I could join it. I plan to see the world and this struck me as a good way to go, at least until our paths diverged."

Robi frowned. "He hasn't mentioned it lately. Come on, I'll walk you back to his office and you can ask."

"Don't you have to oversee the unloading?"

"Nah, the guys know where everything goes. I'm just here as a backup." Robi turned toward the rear of the warehouse and Danny fell in behind him. "So how bad is it?"

"Forte basically doesn't exist anymore," Danny said. "Except as a home for demons and monsters. The little I saw of Guilton seemed okay, but we didn't visit any population centers. As far as the other kingdoms go, I have no idea."

"Damn. I don't know anyone from Forte and thank goodness for that. Here I thought Villipan had a rough time of it. Guess we got off easy."

Danny considered some of the things he'd seen in Villipan and shook his head. "We got it bad enough."

Robi looked back at him. "Want to talk about it?"

"I want to forget it."

They reached the door to Trevor's office and Robi knocked. "Sir? Ronin's here and he wants to speak with you if you have a moment."

There was a squeak followed by the thunk of footsteps then the door opened, revealing Trevor's chubby, bald figure. He offered a friendly smile. "Welcome back. Please step inside."

"I'll get back to work," Robi said. "Drinks tonight?"

Danny nodded. "My treat."

Robi clapped him on the back. "Even better."

Danny followed Trevor into his office and sat in the chair in front of his desk.

"So what brings you by?" Trevor asked.

"Your son's grand caravan. I'm still hoping to join."

Trevor's normally smiling face turned grim. "About that. I fear it may not happen. Last I spoke to him, none of his partners had confirmed their willingness to proceed. Marko only has three wagons of his own and can't afford enough guards to make the trip safely. If no one else is willing to join, he'll have to cancel and hope for better luck next year."

That wasn't what Danny was hoping to hear. "I can't wait another year. Disappointing as it is, given the state of the Five Kingdoms, I can't say the news is unexpected. I'll just have to travel on my own. Might be for the best anyway."

"I'm sorry to be the bearer of bad news," Trevor said.

"Don't worry about it. I'm not the sort to kill the messenger. I'll get out of your hair. I'm sure you have a lot to do."

Danny left the warehouse, pausing only long enough to promise to meet Robi and his team that night at a nearby tavern. First Danny needed to find an inn for the night, then he'd see about buying supplies and a better map. If the grand caravan wasn't happening, he had no reason to delay.

He'd set out for Elfhome first thing in the morning.

CHAPTER 32

L yra couldn't begin to describe how relieved she felt when Villipan City came into view and she found no black dome over it. All the blood, sweat, and pain had been worth it. Nearly as encouraging was the line of wagons at the western gate. They were all piled high with supplies. No doubt the people would be delighted with something other than magic bread to eat. All Lyra wanted was to hug the girls, go home, and sleep for a week. She'd earned that much surely.

She marched down the road at a steady pace until she reached the end of the line of wagons. Ignoring it, she kept going to the gate. The guards were back on duty, six of them in fact. Though they looked a bit pale, their cheeks hollow, and their eyes dark, they'd returned to duty. Lyra respected that.

An older man with a sergeant's insignia on his tabard stared at her as though he'd seen a demon. Lyra no longer took it personally.

"Lady Shael, welcome back," he said. "Was it you that took the dome down?"

"Yes, though I did have help. Unless you need something, I very much wish to enter and report to Prince Florian."

"Right, of course, please, go right through. I didn't mean to delay you."

She waved an exhausted hand. "It's fine, Sergeant. Good to see you and your men back on duty."

With that she strode through and headed for the cathedral. She didn't know if the prince would be there and despite what she'd said to the guard, she didn't care. Lyra wanted to see Tara and Nora.

The city was showing a bit of life. Unlike when she and Daniel left. People were outside, businesses were open, and she even heard some kids playing in the distance. Their innocent laughter was a balm for her weariness. It was like they were saying everything she'd been through had been worth it.

No one troubled her on her walk and soon enough she reached the cathedral. Lyra pushed through the doors and marched into the chapel. Eve was praying before the altar and looked up as she entered. The young woman's face lit up and she hurried over, wrapping Lyra in a hug.

Not at all comfortable with such close contact, Lyra gave her an awkward pat on the back.

"I'm so glad you're safe," Eve said when she finally let go. "I assumed you'd won when the dome vanished. Where's Daniel?"

"He should be in Rosenbar by now. We parted ways after dealing with the priestess. He told me the contract was fulfilled and I couldn't argue considering how much extra he did for us. I'm sure there are still stragglers wandering the wilderness, but for the most part, Villipan, at least, should be mostly safe."

"He's not coming back, is he?" Eve asked.

"No. He's likely already on his way out of the Five Kingdoms. He's chosen his own path and we have no choice but to accept his decision."

"Yeah, but that doesn't mean I can't miss him. You know, right up until this moment, I kind of thought he might change his mind. I understand why he didn't, but still..."

Lyra found Eve's naïveté heartwarming. She hadn't, not for a moment, really believed Daniel would change his mind. She had hoped, but not believed. The fact that he did as much as he did after she'd killed him was remarkable enough.

"Where are the girls?"

"Playing in my room. The royals went back to the castle. All the soldiers and servants collapsed at the same time the dome vanished. The priests have been working steadily to remove all traces of the control magic used on them. Today's my day off, but Sister Rose is there helping."

Lyra nodded. As she'd hoped, things were getting back to normal. "Anything else I need to know?"

"The braineaters escaped. No one's sure how, but they slipped out of the locked cells one night."

"They must've given up their stolen forms."

Eve cocked her head. "How would that help?"

"Their natural form resembles an amoeba. They could squish through the bars no problem. I wonder why they decided to give up their human forms."

"They probably didn't want to be executed. Prince Florian informed them that as soon as the crisis was over he planned to have them beheaded for regicide."

Lyra scrubbed a hand across her face. "Yeah, that

certainly explains it. I knew he wasn't the sharpest sword in the armory, but why in the world would you tell them you planned to kill them rather than just waiting until you were ready and doing it?"

Eve didn't answer and she hadn't expected her to. She was asking herself as much as anything. "I'm taking the girls home. I'll visit the castle tomorrow."

Or maybe next week.

"Sure. It'll be awfully quiet with them gone."

Lyra smiled. "I figured you'd be happy to have your bed back. Seriously though, I can't thank you enough for looking after them. I don't know what I would've done if you hadn't been willing."

"Don't be silly. I would never ignore a child in danger. Go have your reunion. You've earned it."

That sounded like the best idea Lyra had heard in ages. She gave Eve's shoulder a squeeze in passing then hurried back to the cathedral's living area. Her walk soon turned into a jog then a run. When she reached the closed bedroom door she let out a sigh.

After a quick knock she pushed it open. The girls were sitting on the ground playing with crudely made dolls. They both looked up at her, their eyes got wide, and they sprang to their feet. "Grandma!" they shouted in unison.

The next thing Lyra knew she had two little girls wrapped around her. As she squeezed them back Lyra felt the tension leach out of her. They were safe. She was safe. For now, nothing else mattered.

"What do you say we go home?" Lyra asked.

"Can we?" Tara asked.

"Please?" Nora said.

"We certainly can. Let's go." Taking their hands, Lyra led the pair out of the room, back through the chapel.

They paused long enough for the girls to say goodbye to Eve. It seemed they'd gotten quite attached to the priestess and much hugging and crying followed.

When they were done, the trio left the cathedral and turned up the street. As they walked Tara asked, "Where's Daniel?"

"He's gone, dearheart. Off on a mission of his own."

"When will he be back?" Nora asked.

Lyra shook her head. "I don't know if he will be back. Villipan didn't treat him very well despite all he did."

She had no intention of explaining her betrayal to her granddaughters. They were still too young and innocent to understand that sometimes you had to do hard things for the greater good. Or so she justified her actions.

"I miss him," Nora said, sniffing a little.

"Me, too, dearheart, me too."

Lyra was surprised to find she meant it.

EPILOGUE

Danny adjusted his pack and strode through Rosenbar's western gate. The pack wasn't heavily laden—he kept the bulk of his supplies in his personal storage space—but it did have enough stuff to last a few days. Should he run into fellow travelers, it would be far simpler to take what he needed out of the pack. Not that he had any intention of seeking out traveling companions. It was easier to move on his own and at a pace of his choosing.

Drinks last evening with Robi and his team had been pleasant. Now that things had calmed down, they were busy guarding wagons most days. Robi had tried to convince him to join the group and continue scouting, but Danny turned him down. Still, it was flattering to think they wanted him around. Danny was pleased he'd made at least a few friends in this place.

But now it was time to move on. Destroying the summoning circle wasn't going to happen quickly. He didn't have many details about how it worked. All his hopes centered around finding what he needed in Elfhome.

On the plus side, he'd purchased a fairly detailed world map from the Adventurers' Guild. It had the main nations and some of the larger cities along with rivers, lakes, and other natural obstacles. Given the massive scale of the continent, that was about the best Danny could hope for. His plan was to collect more local maps as he went and fill them in. Mostly for his own reference.

He took a deep breath of cool morning air. How did the saying go, the journey of a thousand miles begins with a single step? Well, this was his first step, though he felt certain his journey would be far more than a thousand miles.

○

I n four dark places scattered across the continent, a figure of beautiful terror woke. She lay on a black altar, on a soft feather bed, on a stone floor, and on a platform of frozen blood. Eyes that burned with intensity and a desire for revenge stared at their surroundings. They were all different, some beautiful, others plain. None of the details mattered.

Nearby, worshippers of Ardent Lilly knelt in supplication. They didn't matter either, not really. They were nothing but tools to be used and discarded as the mission required.

All was as it should be. The demon king took a deep breath. She had cheated death. The greatest gamble of her life had gone in her favor.

"The quadripartite resurrection was a success." Four voices in four places spoke as one. "I have returned."

AUTHOR NOTE

Hello everyone,

Danny's time in the Five Kingdoms has come to an end. But don't think that means an end to his adventures. New threats and new adventures await beyond Fell Forest. Join me next time in The Plague Lands to see what the future holds for our hero.

If you don't want to miss any of my new releases, deals, general news about the Etherverse, you can signup for my newsletter on my website.

www.jamesewisher.com

Until next time, thanks for reading,

James E. Wisher

Overmage

The Divine Key Trilogy
Shadow Magic
For The Greater Good
The Divine Key Awakens

The Portal Wars Saga
The Hidden Tower
The Great Northern War
The Portal Thieves
The Master of Magic
The Chamber of Eternity
The Heart of Alchemy
The Sanguine Scroll
Shadow of The Dragons

The Dragonspire Chronicles
The Black Egg
The Mysterious Coin
The Dragons' Graveyard
The Slave War
The Sunken Tower
The Dragon Empress
The Dragonspire Chronicles Omnibus Vol. 1
The Dragonspire Chronicles Omnibus Vol. 2
The Complete Dragonspire Chronicles Omnibus

Soul Force Saga

ABOUT THE AUTHOR

James E. Wisher is a writer of science fiction and Fantasy novels. He's been writing since high school and reading everything he could get his hands on for as long as he can remember.